SOYANGRI
BOOK
KITCHEN

SOYANGRI BOOK KITCHEN

KIM JEE HYE

**TRANSLATED FROM THE KOREAN BY
SHANNA TAN**

HARVILL

1 3 5 7 9 10 8 6 4 2

Harvill, an imprint of Vintage, is part of the
Penguin Random House group of companies

Vintage, Penguin Random House UK, One Embassy Gardens,
8 Viaduct Gardens, London SW11 7BW

penguin.co.uk/vintage
global.penguinrandomhouse.com

Penguin
Random House
UK

First published in Great Britain by Harvill in 2025
First published in South Korea with the title 책들의 부엌 in 2022
by Sam & Parkers Co., Ltd, Seoul

Copyright © Kim Jee Hye 2022
English translation copyright © Shanna Tan 2025

The moral right of the author has been asserted

This book is published with the support of the
Literature Translation Institute of Korea (LTI Korea) and the Toji Cultural Foundation

Extracts from Maeve Binchy's *A Week in Winter*, Ito Ogawa's *Tsubaki
Stationery Store* (translated here by Shanna Tan), L. Frank Baum's *The Wonderful
Wizard of Oz*, Delia Owens's *Where the Crawdads Sing*, L. M. Montgomery's *Anne of
Green Gables* and Kaori Ekuni's *Butterfly* (translated here by Shanna Tan)

Typeset in 11.1/15.2pt Calluna by Six Red Marbles UK, Thetford, Norfolk
Printed and bound in Great Britain by Clays Ltd, Elcograf S.p.A.

The authorised representative in the EEA is Penguin Random House Ireland,
Morrison Chambers, 32 Nassau Street, Dublin D02 YH68

A CIP catalogue record for this book is available from the British Library

ISBN 9781787304628

SOYANGRI
BOOK
KITCHEN

PROLOGUE

As the sun rose, the early morning sleet on the bare branches of the plum blossom trees melted into a glistening sheen. Under the pale sunlight, the surroundings seemed to brighten. While winter still held a tight grip, fresh spring air was beginning to seep through its cracks, heralding a new season.

It was two in the afternoon. Yoojin, who was inspecting the tiling work, suddenly looked up. A sweet, somewhat distant fragrance was drifting in from the windows which she'd opened as wide as possible to air out the smell of cement and paint from the new building. Outside, the trees, which stood firm, rustled their pale green leaves in greeting. Clusters of tight blossom buds hung from the shaded branches, while the ones that basked in the sunshine were plump with water, their droopy heads rising like children stirring from a nap.

Yoojin walked over to the windows. With a gentle push, the brand-new insect screen glided open with ease. The wind from the mountains rushed in, filling the room with its subtle scent. Her gaze landed on the snowflake-like petals, and she realised with a start that it was her first time seeing plum blossom flowers up close. The petals were the same shade of white as the tiles in Soyangri Book Kitchen, her shop which was almost ready to open. Behind the trees, the white bedsheets she'd washed and hung outside for their 'bookstay'

I

guests flapped in the breeze. Was the scent from the flowers or the fabric softener? She inhaled deeply and relaxed.

Turning away from the windows, her gaze swept over the book café. Being surrounded by bookshelves that took up the entire wall made her feel like she was inside a doll's house of sorts. The LED lights cast a warm glow on the bare shelves, illuminating them like an empty stage.

May the smell of books fill this space.

She glanced at the A3-sized paper taped to the wall. The floorplan for the book café was filled with markings and tiny notes scribbled on the side, reflecting the countless rounds of revision and the careful thought that had gone into it. The crumpled edges gave it a worn look, making it seem out of place when everything else was brand new. Yoojin stretched out a finger and rubbed gently on a pencilled scrawl. What had once been just a floor plan and a 3D simulation model on the computer was now the building she was standing in.

In addition to the bookshop, which doubled up as a café and event space, Soyangri Book Kitchen would also be running a 'bookstay': accommodation for those looking for a getaway from the hustle and bustle of life. Of the four two-storey buildings it occupied, three were guesthouses. And the building in which she stood now housed the book café, as well as all the staff on the upper floors. From a bird's-eye view, with a garden and a botanical glasshouse in the centre, the compound looked like a cross.

The book café's floor-to-ceiling glass windows offered a panoramic view of the picturesque Soyangri village. Behind the plum blossom trees, one could make out the meandering mountain ridges in the distance. Gazing at their majestic yet gentle curves, Yoojin sometimes wondered if she was living in a dream. As a Seoulite born and raised in the city, Yoojin was more used to tall, sharp-edged skyscrapers, 24-hour convenience stores, chain cafés, a sprawling subway network and high-rise apartment buildings.

'Yoojin nuna, come check if we've got this on properly.'

From outside, Siwoo called out to her.

'Okay, one second!'

Yoojin closed the insect screen with one hand and stuffed the tape measure into the front pocket of her apron before hurrying outside. Siwoo and Hyungjun were holding a two-metre-long banner across the façade of the coffee kiosk next to the building.

OPENING SOON

SOYANGRI BOOK KITCHEN

Taking reservations from 1 April!

Below the bold letters was a phone number and their Instagram handle.

'Looks good. Wait, let me take a photo,' Yoojin said as she fished out her phone from her apron.

Her shot turned out blurry, but since she was only checking if the banner was straight, she didn't bother taking another one. What she couldn't predict, in that moment, was the regret she'd come to feel several seasons later, when she happened to look back at that hazy shot of Siwoo, his bangs windswept and a wide grin plastered across his face, while Hyungjun wore his usual poker face.

3

Siwoo, her cousin, and Hyungjun, who was born and raised in Soyangri, were her full-time employees. Like two ends of a seesaw, they were polar opposites. Siwoo was an extrovert with a short temper, while Hyungjun was quiet and preferred to keep to himself. It'd be nice if they could find balance in each other, she thought wryly, as she watched Siwoo run towards her eagerly to check out the photo while Hyungjun ambled behind.

'Siwoo, don't you think it's a little high on the left side?'

Siwoo tilted his head a fraction.

'Hmm. The stone foundations of the storage shed that originally stood there weren't level in the first place. Maybe that's why.'

'Hyungjun, what do you think?'

'Looks fine.'

'Right?' The two men high-fived, grinning. Despite their differences, in moments like this, they were like twins with a shared soul.

Yoojin chuckled to herself and turned to survey the place.

Soyangri Book Kitchen sat at the foot of the mountain. The four modern buildings stood out in the rustic landscape, like items that suddenly pop up in a video game. For a moment, she lost her bearings. Where was she? What year were they in? Which day of the week was it? It had been a ten-month journey to build everything from scratch, but it was as if she was going to wake up any moment and not remember a single sliver of the dream.

If someone were to ask her why she had decided to open a bookshop in the countryside, Yoojin didn't have a prepared answer. True, she had often quipped about wanting to retire in a quiet place with greenery and spend her days reading, but never had she quite imagined that at only thirty-two she'd be running a book café, as well as a guesthouse in the countryside.

But from the moment she had decided to buy the piece of land, it was as if she'd been swept up in a whirlwind. She had rushed to complete the paperwork required to register the business, and to pay the deposit she'd sold her 'officetel' studio apartment. Then she had been on tenterhooks waiting for the bank to approve her mortgage loan, before selling off almost all the shares in her portfolio to pay for the necessary permits and begin construction on the site. To obtain the operation licence for a café, she had to undertake the requisite training, and thinking that she should at least know the basics of coffee-brewing, she signed up for barista classes also.

Often, she stayed up till the small hours of the morning to look over the floorplan with the architect firm recommended by Siwoo. Much time and effort had also gone into curating the books for the book café, as well as designing and producing their in-house merchandise, like mugs, notebooks and tote bags. To select the furniture, lights and appliances, she had thumbed through countless interior-design magazines and surfed the internet for inspiration.

Even landing on the name 'Soyangri Book Kitchen' had taken Yoojin two whole weeks. She wanted a name befitting of a place filled with books. Drawing inspiration from the idea that every book has a unique flavour that would appeal differently to its readers, she hoped that by naming the shop a book kitchen, it would become a space where people could enjoy some reading time and rest their weary hearts. Like how food comforts the soul, she hoped, too, that the delicious smell of paper and books would make her guests feel comfortable enough to shed the burden of bottled-up feelings, and to embrace some moments of solace and warmth.

When the flurry of activities had finally begun to settle, it felt as though she'd emerged into a strange, new world.

Suddenly she felt a gnawing hunger. She had barely eaten breakfast, just half an apple and a day-old donut. The books she had ordered were supposed to arrive that morning, so she had planned to wait for the delivery before getting lunch, but it was already past two and there was no sign of them. She had been too busy to register the compound on the navigation maps, so delivery trucks had arrived late on several occasions because they'd missed a turn. Yoojin called out to Siwoo and Hyungjun, who were huddling over a computer tablet, deep in discussion.

'Guys. I'm not sure when the books are coming. Shall we go grab lunch at the city centre and drop by the supermarket? Hyungjun, you can save yourself a trip back and get off work there.'

1
GRANDMA AND THE NIGHT SKY

Da-in spent the three years of middle school attending auditions every weekend. It was about the only thing she remembered doing. While they told her that she had decent vocals, behind her back, she caught whispers that she didn't have the looks to be a celebrity, and it loomed over her like a dark shadow. Da-in knew. Whenever she looked into the mirror and saw the baby fat in her full cheeks, her bare face with only a smear of sunscreen, she couldn't help but think of the gorgeous idol trainees she'd met at the auditions. They hadn't gone under the knife, but their features were exquisite, almost doll-like. Their mere presence turned heads, including hers, as if they were already veteran artists. She wondered wryly if they were from some gifted education programme for stars-in-the-making she hadn't known about.

Da-in was eventually signed to a small record label, but her debut under the stage name *Diane* had largely gone unnoticed. The entertainment industry was churning out tens of idol groups every year, but the harsh reality was that only two or three would make it while the rest would, like cherry blossoms, be forgotten in a few months. It didn't help that Da-in's agency was also new; she was their first artiste. Despite having a couple of employees who'd worked in big-name agencies, it was obvious, from the marketing concept to her stage outfits, that they lacked the resources big labels had. Sometimes it felt like they were in a school club, not a business meeting, when the staff discussions were comprised of questions like 'Maybe we can try this?' or 'I heard other companies do this.' With the air of a casual chat more so than a serious meeting, somehow, they'd concluded that Da-in didn't fit the idol concept anyway. That, everyone agreed.

At that time, the girl group Delicious were all the rage. They were the walking definition of idols. Every member boasted perfect proportions like a Barbie doll, a charming wink, lots of aegyo, and a sweet smile that melted hearts. *No way I could be like them.* Da-in sighed. But if she couldn't be an idol, then what? She could call herself a teen musician, but there was no lack of even younger artistes making their debut. Perhaps *cute* fitted her better than pretty; she could be the cute soloist boasting vocals that would put Mariah Carey to shame. No, that sounded ridiculous even to her ears. And because she didn't write her own songs or lyrics, she couldn't be a singer-songwriter either.

But three years on from her debut, Da-in – as Diane – catapulted overnight to the coveted status of the 'Nation's Little Sister'. She had discovered her greatest skill. She was a good listener but an even better storyteller. The 10 p.m. radio programme, where Da-in was a last-minute substitute for a regular guest, hit an all-time high listenership that night and the radio producer was eager to make Da-in a regular guest too. Within six months, she had added five radio shows to her schedule.

Listeners adored her warm voice, slightly husky but smooth on the ears, and the way she brought stories to life. There was something lovable about her earnest attitude, like a chocolate muffin that, despite best efforts, turned out slightly lopsided but still delicious. She had a knack for putting the guests at ease, her sincerity touching the deepest corner of their hearts. Her live covers went viral on YouTube. There was her perfect rendition of Mariah Carey's 'Hero', a song that demanded explosive vocal power, and her strumming an acoustic guitar while belting out a sweet rendition of Jason Mraz's 'Lucky'.

Her first original track to make it to the music charts was 'Spring Day', an acoustic jazz track about a young woman working part-time at a convenience store who dreamt of travelling to Morocco whenever spring came around. It was the perfect song for her unique vocals – a departure from the formulaic K-pop beat yet maintaining strong mainstream appeal. The song barely received any attention when it was first released, but everything changed after a male idol sang a couple of lines in a variety show. A video of a group of high-school students dancing to the song went viral soon after and when it became the featured track on the latest mobile-phone ad, the song was propelled belatedly to the music charts. Not only did it make the charts, the three-month-old song further defied expectations by climbing the ranks. Riding the wave, her next digital single 'That's Good Enough' claimed the number one spot upon its release and held the crown for a whole month as the music video hit with record-breaking views on YouTube. Endorsements and commercial deals came rolling in for Da-in. Brands started to take notice of her, and suddenly, she was touted as a rising star with a fresh face and flawless vocals.

Now, everyone had heard of Diane. People were recognising her on the street. She became the number one sought-after celebrity, with fellow artists clamouring to collaborate with her. Her fame extended overseas as well; the album ranked high on iTunes Asia. And her fans, which had grown exponentially in number, worshipped her like a god who could do no wrong.

That made her afraid. She was still the same old Da-in, yet the world was treating her so differently. Everyone was lavishing her with praise, calling her talents unrivalled. Carefully, she trod through her newfound popularity. At the same time, she worried that it might burst at any moment like a bubble.

Time flew by. It was now the eighth year that she held the title as a top celebrity – the Nation's Little Sister, Diane. Her fans nicknamed her the human pastel macaron. In her music videos, she twirled around in elaborate floral dresses, capturing everyone's heart with her dazzling smile. Male fans binge-watched her videos to soothe the loneliness of Valentine's Day, and she was the teenage girls' number one role model.

But off screen, Da-in was more comfortable wearing plain hoodies. In the recording studio, she usually kept to herself, a far cry from the bubbly persona in her vitamin drink ads. Even when she was younger, she'd never been an extrovert. She much preferred to retreat into her own world and thoughts. With her parents, she was close, but not overly affectionate. She didn't wear her heart on her sleeve, but in her own way, she was quietly observant and took good care of her loved ones.

Looking at herself on screen, Da-in sometimes wondered if she was being 'fake'. She was deeply afraid that any moment, the public's love and attention would quickly spiral down into criticisms and finger-pointing.

Today was the first time in a long while that she had a whole weekday to herself. She had planned to sleep in, but after a restless night, she woke up lethargic. Until three in the morning, she had tossed and turned in bed, weaving in between anxious dreams.

In one of them, Da-in was late for her radio show. The loud clicks of her heels echoed down the long, narrow corridor. As she ran, the landscape melted away, and the next moment, she was hosting a talk show in a TV studio. She was speaking animatedly, but suddenly, the guests' expressions hardened. Flustered, she tried to keep the show going only to see close-ups of her own face staring at her from every single monitor on set.

Da-in jerked awake in shock. The scene loomed in her mind, yet to fully dissipate. She dragged herself, messy bedhead and bleary-eyed, to the living room and turned on the TV. Her face in flawless make-up popped up. She watched herself smile and chat animatedly on the talk show. When the credits rolled, her MV came on. Was this charismatic woman really her?

Panic gripped her. *I looked like an empty shell.* Being a singer was her childhood dream, but it wasn't like she craved the spotlight. She wanted to express herself through her music, and thought the public had accepted her for who she was. But now, she realised how wrong she'd been. What the public loved was only their idealised image of Diane.

Back in bed, Da-in heard her heart pounding loudly. *Kung kung.* As if a rumbling train was approaching, louder and louder, thundering past her ears. She gasped for breath, as though a dark shadow had its fingers wrapped around her neck.

The next thing she knew, she fell into another dream. She was pressing her nose against the glass enclosure like a beast on display. One moment, she was a monkey, entertaining children with her antics. Then she was a waddling king penguin. Office workers in their twenties squealed at the sight of her. In the next scene, she had morphed into the most popular animal in the zoo – the panda – a perpetual smile plastered on her face. A 360-degree view of her every action was live-streamed on the internet. Like in a video game, the audience had full control selecting her outfit, the colour of her fur, the accessories. Da-in was completely at their mercy. There was no room for her feelings. The shock, sadness or anger. The loneliness.

***

Da-in missed her grandmother. Unlike her, Grandma lived life with a healthy dose of optimism. Even on a rough day, all she'd need to do is take a walk outside, soak in the sunshine and she'd be able to brush off the unhappiness. Da-in had never seen huge waves of emotions roll off her; she was always like a little boat cruising down a calm river.

Da-in missed the warmth of Grandma's hands. Whenever Da-in found herself plagued by insomnia for more than a week, she'd turn up at the doorstep of her grandmother's traditional hanok house, and she'd be there to receive her with a kind smile and an affectionate tummy rub. No questions asked.

Grandma never listened to her songs. Even before Da-in became famous, her grandmother's tinnitus had worsened, so she stopped listening to the radio or the TV. Da-in didn't mind. She had more than her share of judgement from other people, be it praise for her amazing new songs or criticism that her voice had weakened since her previous album. Grandma never did that. In her quiet way, she'd lend Da-in a lap to lie on. Grandma's hands were sinewed, but her touch warm.

Next to her, sleep came easily to Da-in. The breeze that caressed the eaves of the hanok, the delicious smell of stew in the house, the dog barking in the distance and the warm orange glow of the sunset gently lulled her into a deep slumber. Whenever she stayed over, she could enjoy ten hours of uninterrupted sleep. And when she woke up, they'd go on long walks in the neighbourhood. From the street sellers, they bought fruits by the crate. When the five-day market was running, they'd shop for loose-fitting floral ajumma pants, and at the neighbourhood restaurant, they'd order steaming bowls of gukbap rice soup – for takeout. Back home, they'd pick some fresh lettuce and green peppers, and from the jangdokdae platform, where earthenware jars of sauces and condiments were kept, they'd scoop out a ladle of red pepper and soybean paste, and mix them with a dash of sesame oil and powdered perilla seeds for a delicious dipping sauce for the peppers.

Coming down to Soyangri was a spur-of-the-moment decision. Grandma was no longer around. Three years ago, she'd moved to the nursing home and last year, she had passed away. Even before then, the hundred-and-fifty-year-old hanok had been sold to pay for her medical expenses. In any case, it was getting too expensive to maintain the traditional house. The hanok structure was subsequently moved to a site with breathtaking views, where it became a boutique hotel two years ago. Over the phone, Da-in's mother had told her that the only thing left on the land was the storage shed where little Da-in had loved playing hide-and-seek.

With only a tiny shaft right below the roof, the shed was relatively dark even at midday. Da-in used to climb into the mother-of-pearl closet behind the messy stacks of old books and bags of rice, and most of the time she would be the last person standing in the game. Even if the seeker popped in to check, all they'd see were the shovels leaning against the wall, the nose rings and millstone from the times her family had kept cattle on the farm. Their eyes would sweep past the piles of paper, the large frames and dusty exercise equipment before quickly nipping out for fear of meeting an enormous spider dangling midair.

OPENING SOON

SOYANGRI BOOK KITCHEN

Taking reservations from 1 April!

Da-in stared at the banner. Below, in a smaller font: *Visit our bookshop café or book a stay with us. May you find encouragement and comfort in our kitchen of books.*

The banner flapped loudly, but Da-in was deep in thought and didn't notice the wind.

She let out a small sigh. If only she'd known earlier, she'd have bought the land, whether it was to build a holiday home, an office, anything. But her dad didn't want her to be trapped in grief.

So, only after everything was settled did she learn that last May, her eldest uncle, who had migrated to the States with his family, and her third uncle, who ran a bed and breakfast in Spain, had flown back to Korea for a short visit. The eight siblings, including her dad, who were usually busy with their own lives, had gathered for the first time in several years to discuss the sale of the hanok and to settle the division of the proceeds. After all, those living had to keep going. Her dad knew about her insomnia, although not her panic disorder, and he'd hoped that Da-in could tuck away the beautiful memories she'd shared with her grandmother, safekeep them in a drawer in her heart and move on. She knew he was deeply concerned for her, so when he only told her after the land was sold, she didn't kick up a fuss.

But she wanted to make a trip here, back to the land where her grandmother's breath seemed to linger. At the foot of the mountain, shaded by the majestic silhouettes of the ridges, the plum blossom trees were beginning to bloom through the darkness of the receding winter.

When nine-year-old Da-in chirped away happily to her grandmother that she wanted to be an idol singer when she grew up, Grandma would smile affectionately at her and ask, 'Shall we get some twisted breadsticks for our afternoon snack?' But now, Da-in wondered if there was more her grandmother had wanted to tell her.

The narrow path, where she used to walk hand in hand with Grandma to the market, was exactly as she remembered it. So were the familiar curves of the mountains. But not these structures. They were alien to her.

The wind whooshed past, cuffing the banner with a low, cold whistle. The hanok that had held so many of her childhood memories had been replaced by four modern buildings with wooden roofs. From where she stood, she could see the spacious terrace on the second floor.

Next to them was a tiny structure that couldn't have been more than two pyeong in size. The rafters were a dark chestnut brown and because of the large glass panels, she had a clear view of the interior. Looking at the coffee machine, the bags of beans, espresso cups and trays, it must be a takeout café stand. What had used to be her grandmother's vegetable patch was now a garden filled with rows of small flower-pots and decorated with teepee tents like a magazine shoot location. The place was stylish and warm, yet Da-in felt a painful squeeze in her heart.

A balmy breeze carried over a sweet scent. She turned and her gaze landed on the plum blossom trees next to the café stand. They looked exactly like how she'd remembered them. Her grandmother had loved those trees. The branches swayed slightly as if in greeting. Before she realised it, she had walked closer.

The takeout café stood at the same height as the trees. The weathered stones supporting the structure looked curiously familiar. Da-in took a closer look. No way! That moment, it hit her that the storage shed from her childhood had been transformed into this glass café. By retaining the base of the old structure and installing glass panels, the owner had given the shed a modern twist, a new lease of life. Da-in cracked a smile as tears filled her eyes.

Da-in wasn't very fond of spring. The flowers flaunting their colours seemed to be demanding that people forget the cold winter, forget death. Spring was supposed to be the season of budding hopes, new goals and fresh starts. But who knew? Maybe spring didn't want to blossom. Maybe it also wanted to remember its past and remain in the deep darkness of winter too. Maybe it was still holding on to the grief even as it fulfilled its seasonal duties.

Like the new buildings catching the reflection of the spring sun, everyone expected Da-in to shine, to dazzle them with her smile. Forget about the old shed, they seemed to be telling her . . . When she learnt that the land was sold, she'd thought that the shed would've been knocked down too.

But it was still here, even if its appearance had changed.

Next to the plum blossom trees, the smooth weathered stones proudly carried the memories of time. Da-in swallowed back tears. She imagined Grandma appearing at any moment, greeting her with the usual, 'Oh, you're here?' Suddenly, she recalled what her grandmother had told her.

Plum blossoms are the most eager for spring. They crane their necks, and when the first whiff of the season appears from beyond the hills, they're the first ones to bloom. But if a cold snap hits and it starts snowing, the wet petals look so woeful it makes my heart ache. But that's also why I love them. Their resilience is infectious, especially the way they aren't deterred and do their best to flower beautifully even in bad weather. Isn't that lovely?

***

'Excuse me . . . are you the author Ms Seo Jina?' Yoojin called out from behind as she set down the big cardboard box in her arms.

To celebrate their opening, they'd invited an author to be their first guest for two nights, and in return, she'd write about her experience. It was part of their marketing strategy to promote their bookstay. Ms Seo had texted that she wouldn't be reaching them until five in the afternoon, but noticing the woman at the entrance, Yoojin thought her guest had arrived early.

The woman turned around.

'Oh, I'm just passing by . . .'

Yoojin stared. Strange. Where had she seen her? Yoojin's gaze slowly took in her delicate features, her dewy fair skin, and the way she made even the most nondescript long black puffer jacket look stylish. Yoojin wasn't a TV obsessive, but her instinct told her this woman was a celebrity. Siwoo, who'd followed behind Yoojin, jerked to a halt.

17

'Diane . . .? O-M-G!'

The box in his arms landed on the ground with a loud thud as his hands flew to his lips. He shook his head vigorously, as if trying to make sure he wasn't seeing things. Da-in flashed him a friendly smile. She was used to people reacting this way.

In fact, Da-in was more surprised that the woman had mistaken her for someone else. She must be the owner of the place, the one who'd bought the land. From the intelligent set of her mouth and her kind eyes, Da-in guessed that she must be the thoughtful, considerate type. Grandma would've also taken to her immediately, she mused.

That moment, it felt as though she'd finally broken free from the shadow stuck at her feet. A small smile lit up her face. Not her usual camera-ready smile, but one of relief.

'This used to be your grandmother's house? Wow.'

'Yeah. Once, I insisted on climbing the persimmon tree in the backyard only to end up falling on my butt. My older sister and I used to go up the mountain in autumn to pick chestnut burrs. We didn't care about being pricked and stayed there till the sun set. Oh, and the number of times we accidentally stepped on cow dung as we chased butterflies and dragonflies in the garden!'

Yoojin felt as though she was getting a glimpse into Da-in's childhood – a young girl who preferred overalls to dresses, climbing up the trees and giggling as she tried to free her foot from a pile of dung.

'I thought I'd feel odd, but it's as if I'm back at Grandma's.'

Yoojin smiled. 'You look really excited, Diane-ssi.'

'Oh, please. Da-in will do. I want to use my real name here. I've done many interviews, and I have a habit of keeping a diary too, but ironically, I rarely get a chance to reminisce about the past. Coming here seems to bring back all the memories. It's almost as if my younger self is tottering around the place right now.'

The aroma of fresh coffee rose from the grey-striped mugs, which sat next to the cinnamon waffles and walnut pound cake that Yoojin had bought from a popular bakery nearby. The sweetness of the pastries complemented the rich flavour of the dark coffee. Da-in took a long sip and looked around, pausing at the trees outside the windows.

'Grandma loved those plum blossom trees. She used to sit on the floor in the hanok, trimming red peppers and shelling beans. The trees stood like a beautiful backdrop behind her. Plum blossoms are the first to bloom in spring. Grandma was the one who told me that . . .'

Da-in stood up and approached the windows, emotions swirling in her eyes as she gazed at the clusters of buds. Yoojin appeared at her side and pushed open the windows.

'I knew right from the start I shouldn't touch them. I got the sense that they've lived here for a long time. Over there, it used to be a shed, right? We kept the base structure and built a takeout café stand instead.'

'You've no idea how I choked up at the sight of the stones just now. The number of times I've hidden in that shed playing hide-and-seek.'

Seeing the shine in Da-in's eyes, a smile spread across Yoojin's face.

'He's the one who came up with the idea of the takeout café – our first staff member, Siwoo,' said Yoojin, gesturing behind her.

Da-in beamed at Siwoo, who grinned sheepishly like a teenager. When their eyes met, he blanked out completely. Yoojin chuckled at his starstruck expression.

Thanking him, Da-in continued with a smile. 'I always

get a good night's sleep when I'm here. I have insomnia. The psychiatrist couldn't pinpoint the reason. For a while, the meds worked, but I always end up lapsing back to sleepless nights. But next to Grandma, I'm always well rested. She moved to a nursing home three years ago and passed away last year . . . Sometimes I still dream of her hanok, the sunlight streaming in, Grandma in her hanbok smiling at me. It was almost as if I could smell the woody scent from the chestnut trees in the mountains, see the beautiful sky and its swirl of purple and red light. But now the house is gone. Just thinking about it fills me with such deep pain and longing that I often jolt awake in the middle of the night and can't get back to sleep again.'

'. . . I see.'

Yoojin knew she hadn't done anything wrong, but that didn't stop the guilt from welling up. Everyone had their own memories they wanted to protect, and unknowingly, she had invaded someone's precious space.

'I understand,' said Yoojin. 'Ever since coming to Soyangri, I feel a lot more well rested, as though someone is soothing me to sleep . . .'

Da-in nodded, smiling. Silence descended as memories filled the air. She could almost feel the lingering touch of her grandmother.

She smiled softly at Yoojin. 'Tell me. How did you end up buying this piece of land? I didn't think anyone would be interested since the adjacent Singil-ri is much more convenient with a new national highway that connects the expressway.'

Yoojin grinned. The small waffle shop popped up in her mind.

***

'Is there nothing else you can try?'

'It's simply too rushed. Today is already 12 May, how could you insist that I find a buyer and ink the contract by 1 June?'

The man who first spoke picked up a cup from the table and gulped the water down as if it were soju. His face flushed red. He was wearing an expensive-looking silver-grey suit, but it looked uncomfortably tight on him. Meanwhile, the woman running the waffle shop kept glancing over, as if wondering when to intervene in case it escalated into a fight.

The red-faced man retorted, 'Didn't I tell you a month ago that this is the only time all the siblings will be able to gather? In fact, I told you three months ago! And once my eldest brother goes back to the States with his family, they won't be back here anytime soon!' He let out a deep sigh.

'We tried our best,' said the other man, who was probably a property agent. He'd been speaking calmly but irritation was starting to seep into his voice. 'I've spread the news far and wide. I left no stones unturned, even contacting my acquaintances from the other provinces. There was someone from Daejeon – a friend of a friend – who seemed interested, and I was telling him all about the land and the neighbourhood. But then he went silent for a week before suddenly telling me he probably wasn't keen . . .'

The property agent looked like he was in his forties. He had a squarish face with big, friendly eyes. Even though it was winter, he was dabbing repeatedly at his shiny forehead. His skin was tanned, perhaps from the strong sun in the country-side. He looked slightly cowed.

'Mm hmm. Shouldn't you talk to several prospective buyers at the same time? It's no easy feat for us to gather at one place. And it's been more than a hundred days since our mother's passing. If we can't settle this right now, it's going to cause an inheritance tussle among the siblings,' complained the man in the suit.

The agent replied, 'I completely understand. We're also trying our best. Like I said, we even reached out to out-of-town buyers. I've set up more than twenty meetings just showing potential buyers the land!' He was gradually losing steam from having repeated himself multiple times.

'So what are they unhappy with?' the man in the suit demanded, dragging his chair as he leant forward.

'Well, they aren't going to tell me the truth, are they? . . . But I suspect that they found the land parcel too big. Honestly, if they're going to build townhouses, seventy-five or even fifty pyeong would be more than enough . . . But we're looking at two hundred and fifty pyeong here . . . And as you know, it isn't as well connected here as the neighbouring town. To get here, you need to drive a kilometre along the winding mountain road to get to the foot of the mountain, and there are no amenities nearby.'

The man in the suit downed the rest of the water in frustration.

For a while, there was silence. Through the wide-open windows, a cool breeze swept in. The kitchen, which had been busy churning out orders, was quiet. The two men ignored the ice-cream waffle on their table. As it melted, the vanilla ice-cream drooped to the side, and until it turned into a pool of liquid, the two ajusshis remained locked in their own thoughts.

Yoojin was halfway through her cinnamon waffle. The shop made the rounds on social media for its thick steak-like waffles, so today she made the special effort to come right at their opening time. The sweetness was a perfect match with the aroma of the coffee. Yoojin thought the place deserved its popularity.

At first, she was just eavesdropping for fun. The ajusshis' voices carried over to her table and the shop was too small to tune them out. She had nothing else to do anyway. There was just the right amount of distance between her round table and their long table that she could comfortably listen in and yet pretend otherwise.

But as she listened, a ripple spread through her heart. It started out as a tiny flap of butterfly wings, escalating into something that shook her core. If she were to describe it, it was like the feeling of jolting awake to her phone alarm. The air from Maisan Mountain that morning still lingered on her trench coat, the gentle sunlight whispering into her ears.

Yoojin straightened up and quickly looked up a few things on her phone browser before opening the calculator app. Her fingers tapped busily on the screen and finally, she arrived at a figure. It wasn't quite in the safe zone, but didn't all adventures require a bit of rash courage? To embark on something new was to take on the unknown risks that came along with it. Yoojin gripped her phone and stood up. Slowly, she walked over to the ajusshis, who were still sitting in silence.

'Excuse me . . . Sorry to disturb you. I'd like to look at the land.'

The two ajusshis exchanged a glance. The real estate agent quickly got up, and in his hurry, he hit his knee against the table with a loud thud, followed by a clatter of cutlery. His eyes were shining in excitement.

'Ah . . . of course! Shall we go now?'

***

'So that day, I went to look at the land, and within a week, we signed the contract.'

Yoojin laughed. Even she had to admit that the story sounded ridiculous. Thinking back, there was absolutely no need for the haste and urgency. Da-in chuckled too.

'Wow, you're really a doer. And it sounds like you met my dad! Hahaha!'

'Wait, what? That man in the silver-grey suit . . .?'

They burst out in laughter. Just then Yoojin's phone vibrated. Someone was calling. She checked the screen – *Ms Seo Jina.* Standing up, Yoojin excused herself to answer the call. The author told her that on the way there, she had scratched a stationary car at the parking lot, and she'd have to make a trip to the garage. Apologising, she added that she wouldn't be able to make it to Soyangri today. Yoojin told her not to worry, and they agreed to make arrangements again.

Yoojin returned to the table. She looked at Da-in, who had her back towards her as she stared out the window.

'By any chance . . . would you like to stay the night? The author who was supposed to be here called to say she can't make it today. We just opened, so there are no other guests.'

To welcome their first guest, everything was ready. Towels, dryer, electric kettle, tea and coffee were neatly arranged in the room, which was kept warm and toasty. Also, they had prepared for the next day's breakfast. Da-in's eyes lit up like a child. Immediately, she took out her phone and made a call. Her manager was alarmed at the thought of her sleeping over alone somewhere in the countryside, but after Da-in explained that it was a guesthouse built on the land of her grandmother's hanok, and that it was safe and yet to be opened to the public, the manager reluctantly agreed.

Da-in was on holiday for the next week. She had planned to leave for Hawaii and had already booked her flights and accommodation. But this morning, she had suddenly missed her grandmother and decided to drive down to the country-side. Yoojin smiled as she heard Da-in giving instructions to her manager to change her flights.

To welcome the author, Yoojin had made reservations at a traditional Korean restaurant nearby. But thinking that it might be inconvenient for Da-in to eat at public places, they decided to cook at the guesthouse instead. Yoojin and Siwoo took out all the ingredients they had in the fridge. There wasn't anything fancy, but it was enough to serve up a table of food. Da-in offered to help with the preparations. Together, they sliced the carrots for the egg roll and diced the radish into cubes to make soup. They were slightly awkward with the knives, like kids playing house in the kitchen. Da-in confessed that she barely cooked on her own; she didn't even know how to make basic egg rolls. She giggled as she broke four eggs into a big bowl, and later, she stood in front of the steaming pot on the stove, her face screwed in concentration measuring the right the amount of soy sauce.

Outside, the sun was slowly setting.

'Is there something you'd like to do here?' Yoojin asked over dinner.

Da-in liked how Yoojin was speaking to her in the more polite jeondaemal. Perhaps because she had debuted at a young age, everyone usually dropped straight to the casual banmal even when meeting her for the first time. Da-in looked at Yoojin before letting her gaze and thoughts drift. Little moments like these could be so beautiful.

Turning back to Yoojin, she answered, 'Not really. During summer nights, Grandma and I used to lie on the floor facing the front garden to stargaze. Looking up at the Milky Way, I often imagined that angels were sprinkling stardust in the galaxy. I miss those moments.'

'I see . . . Unfortunately it's not the right season for it. Even though it's already March, the nights are freezing. We don't want you to catch a cold!'

Disappointment flitted across Da-in's eyes. A moment later, she nodded in quiet acceptance.

'Right . . . It's too cold now.' Her voice trailed off.

'Ah . . .' Siwoo ventured tentatively. It seemed like he'd finally got over his starstruck moment, now that Da-in was looking quite different in a casual grey hoodie.

'I have winter sleeping bags . . . it's just they haven't been washed for a year. Damn, it's embarrassing. Erm, you can use one, but it might smell.' He laughed awkwardly.

The night sky in March was captivating. Tufts of dark clouds dotted the sky; the moon played hide-and-seek behind while the stars shone brightly, indifferent to everything else.

It was an unusually bright night. There wasn't a single streetlamp in sight, but from the second-floor terrace, they could make out the landscape. Under the moonlight, the leaves glistened, and away from the cacophony of the city, the air was filled with the gentle rustle of leaves and in the distance, the calls of birds.

Yoojin pushed herself into the musty sleeping bag, leaving only her head outside. Above her, a sea of stars glimmered. It was one thing to learn that stars filled the sky and another to witness their grandeur with her own eyes. It felt like she was only just beginning to peel back the secrets of the universe after decades on earth. *Will I one day be able to break free from the everyday routine of life and travel to where the stars are? Perhaps the shimmering light is a letter from a planet that has disappeared, the lingering trace of what once existed – an embodiment of a moment in the past.* It was as if the universe was crossing the passage of time to reach out to her.

A comfortable silence enveloped them. Because there were only two sleeping bags, Siwoo let the ladies have them and kept himself warm by wearing a long puffer jacket on top of his winter knitted jumper and laying all the blankets he could gather from the book café on the ground. Acoustic jazz music played from the Bluetooth speaker. The music felt like a light fog hanging in the air, enrobing them. The three of them gazed up in silence; it was like watching a music video of the universe in this chilly early spring night.

Everyone was lost in their own thoughts. Yoojin imagined Da-in and her grandma stargazing right at this spot in the hanok. Da-in reminisced about the moments spent snuggling next to her grandmother in winter, warm like roasted sweet potatoes; the summer nights spent watching the stars with her. In the same moment, Siwoo's thoughts hurtled back to the late hours when he was on the way home from the Noryangjin cram school, looking up at the dim light in the sky.

Da-in broke the silence. 'I've never seen so many stars in my life.'

Siwoo nodded and exhaled a white mist.

'. . . What an incredible feeling,' she continued. 'The stars have always been there. How is it that I've never noticed?'

Yoojin gazed up at the speckled sky, thinking back to the sea of clouds at sunrise at Maisan Mountain.

'Indeed . . . Amazing, isn't it? This reminds me. I didn't quite finish my story just now. The day when I came to Soyangri, before I went to the waffle shop, I watched the sunrise at Maisan. The sky was also brilliant that day. Not quite a sea of stars, but the dark blue sky dotted with lights left me feeling warm and fuzzy . . .'

***

From the peak of Maisan, the world below looked like a deep ocean carrying age-old secrets. The mountain ridges formed a dark shadow; together with the clouds shrouding the landscape, they made an ink-wash painting. In the darkness before the first light, the silence flowed like the calm waters of the sea. Forgotten memories turned into a quiet breeze, caressing Yoojin's neck before dissipating into the air.

The sky was dynamic, ever-changing. Behind the east ridges, the first rays of light appeared, colouring the sky orange. Clouds were plastered above, like a train pausing at its stop. The light mist in the air rose like puffs of smoke. On the other side of the sky, the moon hung in solitude.

As the air warmed, the face of the landscape became clearer. As though the train had resumed running, the world was humming again, and nearby, the birds called out.

As Yoojin watched the sunrise from the observatory deck on Maisan, the fog in her mind cleared, revealing the memories beneath. The meeting room in the co-working space where she used to spend many late nights, now occupied by someone else. The never-ending fights with the upperclassman she'd thought knew her the best. How one by one, everyone set off on a different path, leaving her behind. Like a street swept clean of fallen leaves, as if nothing had happened in the first place. Her thoughts drifted to her start-up office, abandoned, the wine bar in Yeonnam-dong that she'd visited with her senior colleague at the consulting firm, who had tried to dissuade her from leaving the firm to set up her own venture. It had started from a small change, but suddenly she realised how everything, including her past friendships, had now become completely unrecognisable. It was as if she had made it through the darkness to the sunlight, only for it to fade away, leaving behind sad, lonely shadows.

***

'. . . If not for the spectacular sea of clouds at Maisan that day, I'd still be stuck in a rut. The comedic exchange between the ajusshis would probably just be a passing conversation I'd happened to hear, and I wouldn't have taken it to heart. That was my first time at Soyangri. I was a Seoulite through and through, and I thought I'd live out the rest of my life there, too. It was definitely not in my life plans to buy a two-hundred-and-fifty-pyeong piece of land here.' Yoojin smiled.

Nestling a heat pack against her cold cheek, Da-in listened attentively to Yoojin.

'At that time, my start-up had just been acquired by another company, and for two whole months, I was living day by day without knowing what I was doing. Our patents were sold, so it wasn't a complete failure, yet life felt so empty and meaningless. All this time, I'd been looking to the future, hustling hard – coding, making pitch decks. For three years, I never took a single day off. Suddenly, I had so much free time on my hands, so I found myself reaching randomly for a book I'd chucked aside after buying it. It was a novel about a woman who left behind a chaotic life to set up a small hotel in the English countryside, and it follows the stories of her guests from all walks of life over a week in winter. That book stirred a travel itch, and I wanted to go somewhere, even if it was nearby. So I came to Soyangri to watch the sunrise at Maisan.'

The night deepened. It was spring, but the warm weather had yet to find a gap to seep into the cold nights. The chilly wind felt like knives on the skin as the cold, dark moments in her life played in her head. After a moment's silence, Yoojin continued.

'That afternoon, the real estate ajusshi showed me the land, and I thought to myself that perhaps I could be like the woman in the novel. And it felt like the sea of clouds at Maisan were quietly encouraging me.'

Da-in's manager arrived at about midnight. The three of them had just come down from the terrace and were enjoying beers at the book café. Dressed in a long thick puffer jacket with a baseball cap, the manager could pass as a cinematographer. Her features were soft, giving the impression of an easy-going and straightforward person. She'd come with a bag of pastries from Da-in's favourite bakery at Seongsu-dong and a special herb tea blend made by the patisserie. There was barely enough space on the table for the pastry feast.

Letting out a gasp of bliss, Da-in reached for a pain au chocolat. Chewing with her mouth full, she turned to Yoojin.

'What kind of books are you going to display on the shelves?'

Yoojin, who took a caramel rooibos teabag, shook her head as she poured hot water into the mug.

'I haven't decided. Some of the books are taking longer to arrive, probably not until the end of the week. Oh, do you have a favourite book? Or something that you've enjoyed recently . . .'

Siwoo was gazing at Da-in with anticipation. The look in his shining eyes seemed to say: *I'll make sure to read it immediately.*

'*Bright Night* by Choi Eun-young! It makes me think of

Grandma, and I became curious about what she was like as a person, not just my grandmother. Reading it fills me with warmth.'

Next to her, Siwoo was bobbing his head up and down like an overzealous poodle. Yoojin resisted the urge to laugh and instead sipped her tea.

She nodded. 'That's a good one. If you liked that, you could consider reading Go Soori's *We Can Walk in Moonlight.* I love the essay collection, the sentences ooze warmth. Or you could try *Pachinko*.'

'Wow. Did you just come up with book recommendations at the snap of your fingers? I'll make sure to read those. Thanks!'

'I should thank you instead. You're helping me understand how I should recommend books to customers in the future!'

'Siwoo-ssi, what about you?' Da-in asked.

Siwoo spluttered out a mouthful of beer.

'Oh no, are you okay?'

'Er . . . I'm fine! All's good!'

His ears were suspiciously red as he stood up abruptly and disappeared into the kitchen to get some wet wipes. The two of them chuckled. Siwoo laughed awkwardly and sat back down again.

'. . . Erm, the book I'm reading is so thick that it's been a month and I'm nowhere near the end.'

'You? Reading?' Yoojin teased.

'Nuna!' Siwoo protested. 'Of course! After all, I work at a book café. Hmph. Anyway, the book is called *At the Peak of the Volcano*, or something like that . . .'

Yoojin giggled. 'I think you mean *At the Base of the Volcano*.'

The manager nodded. 'The book about architecture? I've heard of it.'

Yoojin clapped her hands together and exclaimed. 'Oh yes! Didn't you major in architecture?'

Da-in's eyes widened in surprise.

'You did? Wow. I fell in love with the movie *Architecture 101*, it even made me consider studying it.'

'Erm, well, I didn't pass my architect registration exam . . . I only majored in it in school. Haha. I can't even finish the book . . .' Siwoo said, to chuckles around the table.

Everyone was envious that Da-in was heading to Hawaii. As they shared their travel bucket lists, the conversation somehow sidetracked into a discussion about Haruki Murakami's short story 'Hanalei Bay', which is set in Hawaii. Yoojin mused that if she were to start a book club here, this was the kind of vibes she'd love.

Was it the glimmering stars? Or the feeling that Grandma's presence lingered here? For the first time in a long while, Da-in thought she'd be able to have a good night's rest.

The room was warm and comfortable. Listening to the whoosh of the wind from the mountains, it was about two in the morning when Da-in drifted off into a deep slumber.

It was a slow morning. Everyone slept in. With no plans, none of them bothered setting an alarm.

A quiet spring rain had started before the sun was up. Long, thin streaks fell gently from the cloudy sky. The wind was frigid, as though winter was still breathing its last; the new sprouts trembled in confusion. Tight buds clustered on the cherry blossom trees as their branches shook. It'd been three hours since sunrise, but the grey clouds were like a blind, and behind, one could only make out the vague silhouette of the mountain ridges.

Mornings at Soyangri Book Kitchen were peaceful and

relaxed. The rain pelted the windowpanes in a steady rhythm, bringing a woody scent from the forest.

Yoojin was the first one to wake up. She went downstairs to the café and made herself a drip coffee. With a knife, she cut a cinnamon roll bought by Da-in's manager into bite-sized pieces and warmed the pastry in the microwave. The smell of cinnamon spread in the air like relaxing jazz music. The warm roll, with brown sugar powder dusted on top, was moist and sweet, and the flaked almonds on top accentuated the aroma and texture of each bite. The place was quiet. Usually she'd put on some music, but this morning, the silence felt fitting. Sweet, and fragrant, just like the cinnamon roll.

Yoojin cleared the table from yesterday. As she washed the dishes, her thoughts wandered to the mysterious, breathtaking sight last night. To think that the sea of stars was hiding above the clouds right now! Their ethereal magic had the power to turn every day into a holiday; even if she was just unpacking the boxes of books at the café, the stars were still shining above in the sky.

Once she was done in the kitchen, Yoojin sat down in front of the boxes which were delivered late yesterday afternoon, and she only had the time to peel off the tape. Spotting Maeve Binchy's *A Week in Winter* peeking from between the cardboard flaps, Yoojin reached for it. It was the book which had given her the courage to start Soyangri Book Kitchen.

Touching the book cover gently, Yoojin thought about Da-in. The Korean cover featured a lovely illustration of teatime – checked tablecloth, coffee in beautiful English teacups and saucers, with a salad bowl next to it. Outside the window was a calming seaside landscape.

Wouldn't it be nice if Da-in could visit a place like this, she thought. Where sounds of the lapping waves filled the air.

Where the cat sat by the window, staring at the idyllic landscape, where red-roofed homes dotted the seaside town like doll's houses. She hoped that Da-in would be able to rest in a picturesque village like this, and when she turned the pages, the characters would greet her with open arms. Perhaps this book had also travelled through the passage of time to reach Da-in. Yoojin flipped through the pages absentmindedly, until she paused at a sentence. It was calling out to her.

> Yes, it's a good place to think. Out by that
> ocean, you feel smaller, less important,
> somehow; it puts things into proportion.

Yoojin slotted a bookmark on that page and wrapped the book in a dark red metallic wrapper. Then she tore off a page from an unlined notebook, cut it into the size of a palm-sized memo, and penned a short note.

I hope you'll find your own shed, and may you hear the waves and feel the familiar warmth of your grandmother's touch . . .

On that rainy spring day, Da-in and her manager left Soyangri Book Kitchen before sunset, the wrapped present from Yoojin tucked safely in her suitcase.

Yoojin and Siwoo watched the car grow smaller in the distance. Yoojin imagined Da-in reading the book in Hawaii as she listened to the lapping waves. She hoped that Da-in would be able to smile genuinely without masking her feelings as she lived a busy life at the peak of fame. That she'd be able to find the time to enjoy a warm meal and a cup of tea, a moment to immerse herself in the world of stories and books amid her busy schedule.

It seemed unbelievable that it'd been less than a day since they'd snuggled in the sleeping bags, stargazing. Just as it didn't seem like it'd only been ten months since that fateful day of eavesdropping on the conversation between the two ajusshis at the waffle shop, Yoojin thought as she looked around at the book kitchen.

She sat down at the same table where Da-in had joined them just yesterday. Suddenly, it felt as though Da-in's grandmother's hanok and Soyangri Book Kitchen had done a baton handoff; her touch still lingered in this place.

Between the tufts of clouds, she could make out the blurred glow of the setting sun. Yoojin got up and pushed the big windows wide open, before doing the same to the smaller ones in the kitchen. It was mid-March – the fifteenth, to be exact. In the twilight, a gentle spring breeze carried the sweet fragrance of the plum blossoms indoors, heralding a new season.

2

GOODBYE, MY TWENTIES

Four years on the hamster wheel had made Nayoon used to working life, but at the same time she was getting sick of everything. Her workplace wasn't bad. In fact, both her job scope and the employee benefits at the tech company were decent. But it was like she'd sunk waist-deep in lethargy. Nothing motivated her; she had no passion for work or the workplace. Was this the slump that everyone had talked about?

If she were to be honest, she only wanted to put in just enough effort to get by every day and enjoy the employee perks. She'd considered moving to a new company, but the thought of it was already exhausting. Was there a need? She didn't have terrible bosses, nor did she hate her work. She was not idealistic enough to believe that switching companies would suddenly make the office feel like heaven. However, she was approaching her thirties, and right now, she was nowhere close to where she'd imagined herself to be at that age.

Thirty-year-old Nayoon should've been a successful career woman. She'd imagined her wardrobe filled with silk blouses and black pencil skirts; a superwoman unfazed by all the challenges thrown at her. But in reality, she'd spent the last four years as the maknae – the youngest – of the team, handling trivial tasks. There was nothing over which she could make the final decision, or handle independently. Most of the time, she followed the SOPs and cleared her work with her bosses.

'We're in the generation of centenarians. Once I hit my fifties, I'd better tread carefully in case I get made redundant . . . then what would I live off? When my children are at university, I'll be fifty-two. Damn. Should I start worrying now . . .?' Manager Yi, who had two sons, sighed deeply as he trailed off. The most common lunchtime topic, besides stock investments and Korea's housing situation, was retirement plans.

'I know right? Most of the executives have an MBA . . . maybe I should start thinking about that . . . or should I try my hand at YouTube editing? Learn a new skill or something.'

Yunyeong, a software engineer who had been in the company for three years, looked solemn.

Nayoon sipped her warm mocha latte topped with whipped cream and set the glass on the table. 'I wonder how much it'll cost to open a café? I fell in love with Spanish home-style cooking on my holiday in Barcelona. Do you think I'll make a profit if I set up a restaurant at Itaewon or Gyeong-nidan street?' She let out a soft sigh. 'Those in specialised careers have it good. They don't need to worry about retirement age . . .'

At her dejected expression, Manager Yi retorted, 'Do you really think so? So many clinics go under every year. And lawyers have to hustle for clients – that's so stressful. And because their earnings depend on the number of clients, they can forget about work–life balance. I have a friend in a big law firm, and just recently, I heard he collapsed because of fatigue and had to be hospitalised.'

After lunch, it was back to the grind. Nayoon checked her to-do list. She had to fill in the annual 'personal work goals' in the HR system by the end of the day. Her retirement plans would have to wait till the evening.

By the time she stepped out of the office, she was too tired to think of anything. Her mind was blank; all she wanted to do was to get to bed. The Q1 sales report due next week hovered over her. A couple of departments had yet to give her their input. She shook her head in frustration.

Scrolling through the delivery app, she ordered her dinner, which she finished while watching a popular drama that had aired recently. Soon, she was getting sleepy. Her laundry was still in the basket and she hadn't decided what to wear to work tomorrow. Thinking about next year's plans right now seemed laughable, to say the least. Anyway, there was still time, wasn't there . . . *In life, everything has its own time.* With that thought, Nayoon drifted to sleep.

***

'Soyang-*ri*? Wait. If that place is a *ri*, isn't it somewhere deep in the countryside? Weren't we just checking out the cherry blossoms nearby?'

Chanwook and Serin giggled. If not for the fact that they were at a busy brunch café, they'd have broken into raucous laughter. The two of them high-fived, as if having completed a secret mission.

'Come on. YOLO. No plans, just go!' said Chanwook, excitement colouring his voice. 'When else we will get a chance to do an impromptu trip again? When we get married and have kids, life will zoom past in a blink.'

It was eleven on a Saturday morning. Nayoon was having brunch with them at a café in Pangyo. Flowing melodiously in the background was a chanson which fit the April vibes. Looking at her frown, Chanwook quickly added:

'Actually, Siwoo called yesterday.'

'What? He did?!'

'Yeah. Finally. After such a long disappearance. He said he's working at a guesthouse in Soyangri. It's been three years since we last heard from him. Let's go find him. I told him I needed to see him in the flesh. Didn't we talk about going on a trip before we hit our thirties? At this rate, we're never going to make it even in our forties. I even borrowed my mum's car. All we need to do is set off!'

He dangled the car key in front of them. Nayoon was still a little miffed that they were changing plans suddenly, but she couldn't help feeling excited too. 'Siwoo, that rascal. Not letting him off the hook this time!'

Serin knew Nayoon was won over. She cheered, bobbing up and down eagerly.

'What're we waiting for? Go go go!'

In the car, Chanwook turned up the volume. The drive turned into a karaoke session as they belted out the songs that had accompanied them through the four years in university. Right now, it was Busker Busker's 'Cherry Blossom Ending'. Since when did it become such an upbeat song? Once the melody came on, the three of them sang along with gusto and broke into peals of laughter.

It was two in the afternoon, and they were on the road. Flowers in full bloom rolled past the car windows. This was the last impromptu trip of their twenties. White cherry blossom petals carried in the wind, like a scene straight out of a Studio Ghibli film. Nayoon couldn't believe that this time yesterday, she was in the office that had the same suffocating silence as a study room, typing away at her desk to update the details and agenda for the weekly meeting next Monday.

She had no idea where Soyangri was, but it didn't matter. Siwoo was there. As long as they could reunite as a four, she didn't care where she was going. Nayoon glanced at her friends. They were all working hard to find their place in life. She thought of Siwoo doing the same in Soyangri. Gently, she greeted the memories rushing back to her – the heady days of twenty-one, twenty-two, twenty-three. Cruising along the winding highway, she felt, for the first time in a long while, a thrill in her heart.

***

Yoojin fell into a dilemma as she watched Siwoo in his golden-retriever energy mode. Thirty minutes ago, Siwoo's best friend from university had called him to say that they'd be arriving in an hour's time. They'd apparently met at the advertising club at university and bonded over days and nights spent gaming at the internet café. Two female friends, whom they'd got close to from the same club, were also coming.

'It's peak season right now; the cherry blossoms are in full bloom. All the rooms are fully booked this weekend. Where are they going to stay?'

'They're basically like family. If it's not too cold, we can pitch tents outdoors. If not, they can bunk with me in my room!'

'Four in a room? Do they know you're planning to make them sleep standing up?'

'Um . . . true, it's a little cramped. But we're probably going to stay up late chatting. We can hang out at the second-floor terrace until then. When it's time to sleep, the girls can take my room. Chanwook and I will make do with sleeping bags and the tents on the terrace. Don't worry! It'll be like camping!'

'Er . . . by tents, you mean . . . *those*?'

Yoojin looked flabbergasted at the three small teepee tents in the garden. Siwoo bobbed his head enthusiastically, adding that since those were one-person tents, it'd be easy to move them up to the terrace. Yoojin looked thoroughly unconvinced.

'Siwoo? Those are décor. They don't come with a mattress or anything. How are you going to sleep in those? Don't forget the terrace is tiled. And the winds from the mountains are going to be freezing, not to mention the dew in the morning . . . Isn't it better to sleep on the second-floor sofa instead?'

Yoojin was already starting to worry. Meanwhile, Siwoo was super chilled about the whole affair. Nothing was impossible to him. They were complete opposites. Yoojin needed everything to be planned in advance while Siwoo would dive into something straight away and only start thinking when he ran into issues. Siwoo cast a glance at Yoojin, who was still muttering about cold tiles and winds, while he slowly started to take out the blankets and extra comforters.

'Nuna, back when you were at university orientation camps, did you sleep on a premium mattress? No, right? We're still in our twenties. Still young and energetic. We're not going to have backaches just because we sleep rough for one night. And if it really doesn't work, we can always sleep in the car. And it's an impromptu trip! Isn't that freaking cool? I don't think they're expecting much. We'll be happy just having a space to sit and chat till late.'

Siwoo spoke in his usual breakneck style as he grabbed the items and bounced up to the terrace. Hyungjun, who had just appeared, quietly helped to move a box of spare light bulbs. Yoojin wasn't a hundred per cent convinced but was a little more at ease. At least they didn't sound like the type of sensitive or thorny guests who wanted to be left alone.

Yoojin dug out two red candles from the cupboard. They were housewarming presents someone had given to her when she moved to an officetel apartment near Gwanghwamun. Because the scent was strong, and the candles were big, it was a little hard to find a use for them and she'd kept them for the past few years. She lit the candles next to the tents on the terrace and plugged in the heater. The wind blew, but the flames danced gracefully.

Siwoo took a few stools from the café to the terrace and was deep in concentration taping the cardboard boxes to turn them into makeshift tables. Next to him, Hyungjun decorated the teepee tents with mini bulbs before helping Siwoo with the boxes. Yoojin retreated downstairs, leaving Siwoo behind looking excited as he focused on adding the finishing touches.

'Wow, Siwoo! This looks amazing!'

The second-floor terrace had been transformed into what looked like the film set of a coming-of-age movie. Chanwook, Serin and Nayoon let out excited gasps. Three teepee tents, each big enough for a child to play inside, were set up on the terrace. Next to them were about ten folded lap blankets stacked up. The heater emitted a warm orange glow, and the mini bulbs illuminated the cosy spot.

'It's been way too long. How's everyone?'

'Siwoo, why so formal? That doesn't sound like you. And damn, do you know how worried we were when we couldn't contact you? Come, get your punishment before we talk.'

Serin and Nayoon put on a solemn face as they each gave

Siwoo a hard whack on the back. Chanwook, who'd been watching quietly on the sidelines, chuckled as he joined them.

'Hey hey, calm down. I knew this would happen. I've come prepared with my peace offerings. Look!'

Siwoo quickly wormed his way out and like a magician about to do the grand reveal, he pulled the blanket to reveal an ice box filled with canned beer and an assortment of drinks. The three of them whooped in joy.

'Why am I hungry again? It's only four,' Nayoon complained.

At the rest stop along the highway, they'd had seafood ramyeon with kimbap for lunch, and bought an assortment of snacks – braised baby potatoes, tteokbokki, sausage and rice-cake skewers, walnut-shaped walnut cakes. But now she was hungry again.

Serin nodded. 'Maybe because we didn't have meat . . . Remember how we polished off twenty servings of grilled pork belly during school club orientation when there was only ten of us?'

'Oh please. Siwoo had probably eaten four servings by himself,' said Chanwook to more chuckles.

Siwoo and Chanwook, Serin and Nayoon became a tight-knit group as early as their freshman year. The three musketeers, or in their case – four. They took almost all their general electives together. When Chanwook and Siwoo were serving in the army, Nayoon and Serin went for an exchange abroad so that they could graduate at the same time.

With two guys and two girls in their clique, many had bet that sparks would fly, but they were simply good friends. They'd hit it off when they were randomly put in the same group at the advertising club orientation camp, and miraculously became soulmates. It wasn't even that their personalities were similar. Not long ago, they did the MBTI test and had a good laugh over it when Chanwook and Nayoon came out as polar opposites.

They graduated, dated outside their clique, went through heartbreaks and periods of feeling lost and finally, they all found jobs. Serin became a freelance illustrator, Nayoon joined the management support team of a tech company dealing with intellectual property. Chanwook became a project manager in the sound team for a gaming company. According to him, he handled all sound effects in the games, but until now, Nayoon still had no idea what his job entailed. Siwoo was studying for the architect registration exam but gave up and switched plans to become a civil servant. Ever since he started holing up in the Noryangjin cram school for the civil service exam, he had basically dropped off the radar.

Slowly, they drifted apart. If they were space explorers, it was like everyone found their own orbits and only occasionally communicated through the space station.

But now that they'd gathered in the same spot, they returned immediately to the heady days of their early twenties. The days of stirring awake on the hard floor of their holiday guesthouse smelling like beer and soju, their faces still swollen from having guzzled too much alcohol, busying themselves in the kitchen as they cooked five packets of ramyeon all at once, adding chopped green onions and kimchi to cure their hangover. The days of skipping classes, sitting below Hangang Bridge with a cheap 9,900 won wine from Emart paired with cheese and crackers, spending a leisurely autumn afternoon together. Flashing past like a film scene, Serin and Nayoon quietly wiping their tears on the bus home after visiting Chanwook on his day off at the military base, where they watched him inhale pizza and fried chicken as if he'd never seen real food before.

Over the sizzling grilled pork belly and cans of beer, they reminisced about their university days, and when they looked up, night had already fallen. The spring wind in April was cold, but not cruel. Inhaling the spring night air reminded them of how they'd stayed up at university team-building camps. The familiar temperature and mood put a smile on their faces. Soyangri had a different vibe at night; it felt as though the mountains were closer, and when the wind blew, it brought along the strong forest scent that slowly melted in the air, mixed with the smell of earth, spring flowers and the candles.

Siwoo thought back to the nights in early spring. Compared to a few weeks ago, the air was now gentler, warmer. The sky was dark, but not too dark, as if veiled by a thin layer of fog. A few stars speckled across the sky, like a neatly written hand.

'Namwoo oppa is getting married this autumn.'

It was around midnight when Serin suddenly spoke, her voice devoid of emotion. The three of them exchanged silent glances. Namwoo was Serin's first love. They had broken up twice but found their way back together each time. It had only been two springs since they had broken up for what looked like the final time. Nayoon put down her can of beer.

'He told you he's getting married? When? Who's the girl?'

'His fiancée is a junior from the design team at his company. And nope, Oppa didn't tell me himself . . . I heard it from one of our mutual friends. Actually, I know who she is. She's about a year younger than us and joined his company three years ago right after graduation. I even saw her in person once. Well, they seem like a good match.'

Her tone was calm. She was past the days of being spurred

by jealousy, having to stay out all night to ward off the competition, to revel in the triumph of being Oppa's favourite girl. No longer would she bawl her eyes out like a child who thinks the world is coming to an end, or to scream wildly at the flames of young love.

'Aigoo. Who cares about him. The grief he gave you . . . Hmph. Let's see how well his life will turn out! But when did you hear about it? Why didn't you tell us?'

'It's the kind of thing that's easier to talk about when we're having a quiet moment like this . . .'

Nayoon patted Serin's shoulder as Chanwook and Siwoo knocked cans and drank the last mouthful of beer before crushing them.

Chanwook let out a sigh. 'Honestly, I don't know if I'll ever get married. I don't feel ready at all. Yet it feels like I'm *supposed* to start a family.'

Nayoon, who'd been munching on a snack, sighed. She absentmindedly stirred the simmering pot of fish-cake soup.

'I know right? It's a terrible feeling, like how when our university entrance exams were around the corner yet we barely revised.'

Serin pulled the shawl closer and leant against Nayoon's shoulder.

'Talking about university entrance exams, I wonder if our lives would be different if we were to sit them again now . . .'

Nayoon knocked her can against Serin's and took a gulp.

'I'm getting goosebumps here, Serin. Just the other day, I was having the same thoughts. If I had studied hard enough, would I have made it to the college of oriental medicine?'

Chanwook, who was watching the candle flame dance, chuckled. He glanced at Nayoon as he pulled the tab of a new can of beer.

47

'Oh please. That was a lifetime ago. Wake up. Even if we scrimp and save our salary, we can't even afford the rent of a one-person studio, not to mention a family apartment. That's the reality of the country we're living in today.'

'True, the housing situation is the worst.'

All of them raised their cans at the same time.

'. . . But are you really okay?' Chanwook cast a glance at Siwoo, who'd been quiet and nodding along.

'What do you mean?'

'To give up taking the civil service exam. Didn't you spend three years in Noryangjin surviving on instant meals? Maybe this time's the charm?'

Chanwook felt sorry for Siwoo. He was such a bright, people-loving character, but to prepare for the administrative ninth-grade civil service exam, he cut off contact with almost everyone and studied intensively for three years. Chanwook had been thinking that when Siwoo called to tell him the good news that he had guaranteed job security, he'd chide him for disappearing on them. He had no idea that Siwoo had given up on the exam and come to the countryside.

'The exam is notoriously hard; it's inhumane. Three compulsory subjects and two elective subjects. Basically, if you can't solve the problem within a minute, you're bound to run out of time. Most people can't finish the paper.'

A frown that didn't suit him distorted his features, and as if to shake off the trauma, he shook his head.

'Anyway, being a government employee probably isn't for me. *A kind and upright person who prefers to work quietly at the back end, unnoticed.* Only someone like that would thrive in a government administrative job; that's not quite who I am.'

The three of them stared ahead, as though unsure if the statement was rhetorical. Siwoo must've spent many lonely nights fretting. It was probably the largest tsunami to hit his happy-go-lucky life. It wasn't easy to come to terms with the realisation that positive thoughts don't necessarily lead to ideal outcomes. What had been on his mind when he realised that the hard work in the past three years had gone down the drain? To gather the courage to break the silence and call Chanwook, how much had he grown as an adult?

'This piece of land was basically left deserted for three years. I've journeyed along with this place, witnessing how it turned from an empty site to the Soyangri Book Kitchen that it is now. When the last of the renovations were completed, I looked at the guest rooms, the book café, and in that moment, it was as if I was reborn. I can finally put my roots down and be truly myself here.'

'. . . Oh yeah, it feels like coming full circle, doesn't it? Getting to apply what you've learnt in architecture,' Serin said.

'Yeah. Back then, at twenty, my dream felt childish and unrealistic, but now I know better. Dreams are never meant to be realistic; it's the energy that spurs one to be a better version of themselves. It's the voice that whispers in your ear when you're lost in the labyrinth of life. That's what dreams are.'

'Siwoo . . . have you been taking drama lessons here at Soyangri? You sound so . . . cheesy,' exclaimed Nayoon.

Serin giggled as Chanwook roughed up Siwoo's hair. Nayoon chuckled along, looking at her friends fondly. They fell into a comfortable and familiar silence. True, they were no longer bright-eyed twenty-year-olds. They had their own lives, but gathering like this once in a while was a huge source of comfort. Chanwook opened a bottle that he'd bought at the mart on the way here. The sweetness of the wine spread in the air, mixing with the scent of the cherry blossoms.

He poured out some for Siwoo.

'Cha Siwoo! Buddy, I miss you. Even if you've become cheesier, it's so good to see you again.'

'Damn! I'm feeling the weight of my age!'

'Can't believe we're thirty soon!'

Serin pretended to tear her hair out in frustration. It was a bittersweet feeling, because they weren't sure if who they were now fitted with what their thirties should look like.

'When the flowers come to bloom again, we'll have crossed over to our thirties,' Chanwook said, sounding like he was reading the last lines of a novel.

'It's not the time to be sentimental. The flowers are going to keep blooming even when we're a hundred. Here, cheers!' Siwoo said as he grabbed the bottle from Chanwook and poured himself another generous serving.

That night, Nayoon had a dream. Chanwook was walking down a path lined with cherry blossom trees before crossing a white bridge. He held the hand of his bride-to-be in a white mermaid wedding dress. Like a boundary of sorts, once he crossed to the other side, she could sense that he was never returning again.

Everyone was applauding and cheering. Nayoon, too, but deep in her heart, she couldn't help but feel like it was the end of the four musketeers. As petals rained down, Chanwook was no longer here with them. But Nayoon wasn't prepared to cross to the next stage of life. Her thirties were like the rising tide washing over her, but she could only stand unmoving, watching his back grow smaller in the distance.

***

'Nayoon! Wake up! We said we'd watch the sunrise and cycle by the lake! We're going to miss it if we don't leave soon.'

'Ah . . . count me out.'

'No! You promised yesterday.'

'. . . But we only got to bed at three. I barely slept.'

'I don't care. Hurry up! Here, take your hat!'

Serin shook her awake. Nayoon mumbled okay but drifted back to sleep. In the end, Nayoon was dragged out, with the hat jammed on her head, and packed into the back passenger seat in Siwoo's truck. As the truck travelled past the rows of trees, the branches remained still in the quiet morning. Last night, they couldn't quite make out the landscape, but now they could see the mountains that surrounded the place like a folding screen. The first rays of light had appeared, turning the sky a clear and gentle blue.

The clock on the dashboard indicated 6.11 a.m. Winter might have passed, but staying outdoors until three in the morning in the cold spring came at a price. Nayoon was aching all over. There was a dull throb at the back of her head, with the occasional sharp wave of pain that came and receded. She longed to return to a warm and soft bed. Curled up like a cat next to her on the backseat was Serin, who leant to the side and closed her eyes.

The lake was bigger than they'd thought. It was as if they were looking at the ocean. They could barely make out the opposite bank, and without a wisp of cloud in the sky, it looked like a scene from a postcard. Behind the mountain ridges, the sun was slowly rising. The gentle ripples on the water gleamed in the light, and as the leaves rustled on the tall, sturdy trees, it was as if the sunlight was dancing. Looking at his friends' awestruck faces, Siwoo wore a satisfied smile and bobbed his head up and down.

Nayoon was soaking in the lovely view when she heard soft singing behind her.

'Happy birthday to you, happy birthday to you, happy birthday dear Nayoon, happy birthday to you! Happy twenty-ninth!'

Serin was carrying a cake made of stacked chocolate-coated *Oh Yes!* snack cakes, decorated with Pepero chocolate biscuit sticks and covered with Yoplait yoghurt. Chanwook helped Nayoon put on a birthday cone hat and party glasses shaped like two cupcakes. Siwoo cheered as he pointed his phone camera at Nayoon.

'Did you buy these at the petrol station when you said you needed a bathroom break?'

Nayoon chuckled. She was touched at the surprise; the little things that she'd found odd now made sense. She committed this precious moment to memory, taking in Serin's white sneakers, Chanwook's bedhead, Siwoo's grey sweater. She looked at each of them in turn. The dreamy vibes made the moment almost unreal.

Nayoon blew at the Pepero sticks as though they were candles, grinning hard to keep the tears at bay. She stole a glance at Serin, and as expected, tears were beginning to well in her eyes, while Chanwook was being his usual calm self. Ever the prankster, a mischievous glimmer darted across Siwoo's eyes as he quickly dipped his finger into the yoghurt, smeared it across Nayoon's cheek and ran away.

When would they be able to do this again? She had no idea. But against the folding screen-like curves of the biscuit cake's ridges, the memory of her good friends singing 'Happy Birthday' seemed to live on. Far into the future, she'd still be able revisit this moment fondly. And that was enough for Nayoon.

As they cycled around the lake, cherry blossom petals gently rained on them like the spring drizzle. The outlines of the mountains on the other side of the lake sharpened as if rising onto a stage. Fluffy white clouds that dotted the sky cruised past with the wind. Soon, the sun was fully up. Warm sunshine streamed down. The sky was a perfect blue, as though she was seeing the sky through a camera filter.

Nayoon's thoughts turned to Daeseongri, a popular spot for university orientation and team-building camps. There was a lake there too. She must've been . . . twenty back then, sitting on the raft splashing water at the other boats with her paddle, giggling as a bird she couldn't name squawked and took flight. Those were the days when nobody would ask where she worked, her designation . . . and of course, no reports or weekly meetings.

Like an empty suitcase, the four of them had no plans in life at all. They spent entire days lazing around doing nothing, at times feeling lost at their freedom. On occasion, looking fondly back at their high-school days.

When they stepped into the working world the times spent at Daeseongri felt like a fantasy. Nayoon worked hard, as though trying to prove her worth for every cent she was paid. At first, she stumbled her way through navigating the sales reporting system at work, learning how to use the correct technical jargon in her write-ups. When she didn't manage to book a meeting room in time, she'd bite her nails in anxiety. When her bosses were away on holiday, she fielded calls from the suppliers and partners with hands shaking from anxiety, and in meetings where she had not an ounce of decision-making power, she could only diligently take down notes and then circulate them to the team. That was how she spent each day, like a baby learning to crawl for the first time. By the time she realised it, she was at the end of her twenties. Where had the time gone?

Nayoon pedalled hard. Memories and moments swirled in her mind, as if she couldn't quite find the right drawer for each of them. Sometimes she was about to recall something only to watch her memories become clouded over in the next moment. She eased up on the pedalling as the bicycle cruised down the slope and she turned lightly around the bend. The whirl of the bicycle chain and the whoosh of the wind built up like the crescendo of a musical. Ahead, the blue sky stretched out jovially.

**

'Nayoon, want to write a letter to yourself? We're running a letter-writing event at the book café.'

'. . . A letter?'

'Yep. You can write something, and it'll be delivered on Christmas Eve with a copy of *Tsubaki Stationery Store* by Ito Ogawa. If you don't have anything to tell yourself, you're more than welcome to write to me.'

Nayoon raised an eyebrow. It'd been a long time since she'd had a dose of Siwoo's brand of humour. Siwoo grinned before disappearing, as Yoojin was looking for him. Chanwook and Serin had gone to the mart in the next village and would be back in an hour or so.

She picked up the brochure of activities.

Letter writing service with Poppo-chan
from Tsubaki Stationery Store
(Or in this case, write a letter to yourself)

We'll deliver the letter and the book to you
this Christmas Eve

Below were further instructions in a small print. It would cost 25,000 won to participate. The price included a copy of the book, the paper, envelope and postage. It was also possible to send the letter and the book separately, to different people, and should the participant wish, they could provide the details on the other recipient and the outline of the greetings, and the book café could write the letter on their behalf.

Any other day, Nayoon would've put back the brochure. The thought of writing herself a letter had never crossed her mind. But she'd just spent a lovely night enjoying the mountain winds, watched the lake glisten in the first rays of the day, cycling along the banks as cherry blossom petals fluttered down. Somewhere in her heart, a ripple was beginning to spread. As if Nayoon on holiday had something to say to Nayoon in her everyday routine.

First, she had to choose the paper, the pen, the wax, then the seal before selecting the envelope and the stamp, just like in the novel when a customer asked Poppo-chan to write a letter on their behalf. Her eyes swept across the wide selection of paper in different thicknesses, textures and colours. Nayoon took her time to browse. Back in middle school, she used to write in a sky-blue diary which she'd exchange with her friends every day. They called it the Friendship Notebook. Back then, she wrote with a marker and the ink would seep through the page, making the next page useless. One by one, she touched the papers to get a feel for them.

She favoured a slight thickness in her letter paper. A shade of pink would be fitting for spring, and as for the size, something that could slip into an envelope easily with three folds. She loved the smoothness and the elegance of the traditional hanji paper, but in the end, she went with a light pink letter paper with an illustration of fluttering cherry blossom petals on the top right corner. The paper wasn't thick, but she could tell, from the fact that it was hard to fold the paper without pressing down on it, that it was good quality. As for the envelope, she chose a stiff, simple one with a thin gold border where she could fill in the address. Once she slipped in the letter, it'd look and feel substantial in her hands.

Surprisingly, it didn't take that long to decide on the pen. She'd go with a yellow Lamy fountain pen. She tested it. The ink was a beautiful navy blue, and the nib was of the perfect thickness. Because she'd never written with a fountain pen, at first the nib felt scratchy. She tried to adjust the angle of her grip, and then the ink flowed out smoothly as if a door had opened.

What should she write? Her thoughts were all over the place. But since she was writing to herself, it shouldn't matter if her words weren't the most polished; she wasn't showing it to anyone. Treating it as a diary entry would be good, she thought. After all, all she wanted was to keep a tangible memory of this moment.

Nayoon turned away from the stationery table and entered the small room on the right. At first, she could still hear the ambient noise and the faint jazz music filtering from the main café space, but slowly, like turning the volume down on the radio, all became quiet as she focused on the task. She hadn't expected to come on this impromptu trip, just as she hadn't expected to be writing a letter to herself and using a fountain pen for the first time. She hadn't planned out what to write, but the pen waltzed across the letter paper as if it knew exactly what to do.

She folded the paper neatly and slotted it into the envelope. It puffed up slightly like a robin. The thought brought a smile to her face. Carefully, she melted the wine-coloured wax over the candle, poured it out on the envelope flap and pressed down the seal. She'd selected a cherry blossom pattern inscribed with the words SOYANGRI BOOK KITCHEN forming a circle around the petals.

She slipped it through the letterbox slot and heard a soft thud. Next to it was a quote from the novel *Tsubaki Stationery Store.*

> The letter slipped into the box with a soft *thud.*
> Safe journey, my words.
> It feels as if I'm sending off a part of me.
> I'll wait in anticipation for a reply.
> May this letter reach QP-chan safely.

It'd been a long while since she'd had a conversation with herself. All this time, she'd been suppressing a vague sense of anxiety, fear, alienation, fatigue and regret that would come over her in waves. After a long day of being on her feet at work, all she wanted to do when she got home was to fall back onto the bed. She was too exhausted to even process her feelings, but at times, she felt sorry for herself for living in fear of being lost in her emotions and so not daring to take a step forward on any path.

But now, she had something to look forward to this Christmas. How would it feel to read a letter from her spring self in the festive winter season? She tapped the letterbox lightly. It felt as if she was understood. A melody played in her head, the chansons from the brunch café the day before. More moments flashed past: drinking beer at Soyangri Book Kitchen and chatting all night. The surprise birthday party. Cycling along the beautiful lake.

Nayoon looked out the window. Serin and Chanwook were walking back, their arms full of groceries from the mart.

Noticing Nayoon, Chanwook waved. He wore the same shirt from yesterday, now creased in several spots. There was even a smear of what looked like dirt on his sleeve. Serin raised both arms and waved her shopping bags enthusiastically as her beige dress flapped gently in the wind. She leant forward a little, as if wanting to know what Nayoon had been doing alone at the café. Siwoo, who had run out to help them with the bags, seemed to be explaining something as he gestured towards Nayoon.

The spring sunshine cast a warm glow on their faces. Nayoon also waved hard from inside the café. She had a strong feeling that this memory of the four musketeers would be imprinted in her mind, down to every little detail: the weather, the air, and the surroundings.

Serin had no idea, right then, that in the coming summer, she'd be joining the Soyangri Book Kitchen family for the next few years. With no idea that this place would soon become part of her daily life, she turned back several times as they were leaving, as if hoping to linger for a moment longer. On their way back to Pangyo, everyone sat in silence.

3

THE OPTIMAL ROUTE
VS THE SHORTEST ROUTE

Sohee had a carefree childhood. Her parents, both professors at a local university, always encouraged her to follow her heart. They didn't make her go to an English kindergarten and when everyone else was busy attending cram-school classes, she spent her after-school hours holed up in the library reading. Sohee was a voracious reader, and she loved books from all genres. To her, the world of the printed word felt even more vivid than real life.

In books, she found freedom, more so than in her dreams. She loved adventure stories. One moment she could be an explorer meeting aliens in a never-ending stretch of desert, and next she was a scientist studying the flora and fauna of the Amazon rainforest. She journeyed with the books to the vast universe, wandering among the seven wonders of the world. Books were like a time machine that weaved through the multiverses of time and space, guiding her to explore the mysteries and wonders of earth and beyond.

But from the chats with friends, consultations with her teachers, what she'd overheard in conversations between her friends' parents and the things she picked up from the news, the overbearing pressure of wider society gradually seeped into her. She became aware of the hyper-competitiveness around her, the need to be the best to survive. She learnt the importance of setting yourself apart from others, to be at the top of your game.

'Sohee, you have the potential to go even further.'

'You know it'll be twice as hard to pull up your grades the moment you slip up, right?'

'The world only remembers the number one. So aim for the top. Sohee, you've got this!'

By the time the summer holidays came around in Grade 8, Sohee felt strongly that she was nothing if she didn't finish first in her class. As for what she wanted to do thereafter, she had no idea. All she knew was that she didn't want to lose.

For as long as she could remember, her dad had always been a tenured professor. But it was only when Sohee was in middle school that her mum finally got promoted. It hadn't been an easy journey for her. Unlike her dad, who became a tenured professor right upon returning from his PhD in the States, her mum didn't have the option to study abroad as she had to take care of Sohee. After completing her PhD in Korea, it took her another seven years to make it as a tenured professor at the local university. Their jobs were stable, but there wasn't much room for progression in their career. Whenever she read the lingering regret on their faces, she became more determined not to lose out in the rat race.

She was smart, and perhaps driven by this new obsessive desire to win, she consistently topped her cohort throughout her three years in high school and got accepted into the political science and diplomacy department at a top university in an early admissions cycle. Four years later, she went on to do a Master of Law at the same university. Every exam season was like fighting a war of tenacity and nerves, and all she remembered was the strong smell of traditional herbal medicine that kept her going in the battlefield. Still, despite all the stress, she quite enjoyed her time in law school.

In the summer break of her sophomore year, she received a job offer from a major law firm, and in the first semester of her third year, she passed the exam to be a judicial researcher, scoring another ace in her hand. She mulled over her options, and in the end decided to start off as precisely that: a judicial researcher.

The workload was heavier and the scope wider than she'd expected. In real life, the cases weren't as straightforward as the ones she'd studied in class. She got to experience first-hand the huge volume of documents to be read and processed; she'd thought her seniors were exaggerating at the drinking sessions. The doors of the judges' offices were always closed, while the rest of the staff, buried behind their computer screens, worked in absolute silence. The loudest sounds were those of the thick stacks of documents belong loaded onto book trolleys and wheeled to an office somewhere.

They didn't have the usual workplace culture of team dinners. Everyone got off work at their own time. It wasn't just the judicial researchers. Her classmate, who'd just completed the practical training for prosecutors, complained that it was like being back in the military again. The Court was like the republic of individualism. Everyone was too busy for break times or to play the ladder lottery game to decide on trivial matters like afternoon snacks, and of course, nobody had the mood or the time to explore good restaurants in the area during lunchtime.

But she liked it there. After she sieved through and processed the stacks of documents, the information organised itself in her head. As the outline of the case and its details started to sharpen, she could feel the moment of crystallisation as everything came together. Her tiny work desk was like a small, deserted island, and she enjoyed the quietude that filled her day.

The three-year term as a judicial researcher flew by, and she was now in her third year working as a lawyer in a small law firm in Seocho-dong, part of the busy greater Gangnam area. Next year, she'd hit her seventh year in her legal career – the minimum requirement to be appointed as a judge. She was going to apply next autumn, and if it all went well, by the following spring, she'd be wearing the judge's robes.

Choi Sohee (34), Judge.

Life was moving smoothly like a conveyer belt. She had her life planned out, and she was on track to achieving every single milestone. Until the day she found out . . .

***

Next to the mountain of documents were four thin sheets of paper. Sohee stared unblinkingly, as if she was going to bore a hole into them. There was no need to unfold the papers. She'd already called to confirm their contents, and just yesterday, she'd read them from top to bottom at least five times, not missing a single full stop – the same, thorough way she read the court documents.

She took another glance at them before she sank heavily into the black leather sofa next to her desk. There was a soft *whoosh* of air as she sat down, before silence wrapped itself around her once more. On her desk was a mess of documents for the hearing three weeks later – the evidence, recordings of interviews, petitions. And the empty smoothie cup from yesterday evening.

Sohee took a deep breath and exhaled, closing her eyes. She needed a moment. The air in the office was still. Outside, she could make out the greyish outlines of the street. She felt a numbness in her, alongside a rising urge to take a trip somewhere, even if she had no idea where. In the past seven years, not once had she taken a day off, much less gone on a holiday.

As if guided by her subconscious, Sohee opened the Instagram app. She typed 'forest guesthouse' in the search bar and scrolled through the images and clips. Then she tried the same with 'countryside book cafe' and 'countryside guesthouse'. Her fingers paused. Something had caught her eye.

Book a healing stay with us in the countryside

Soyangri Book Kitchen is running
a promotion for one-month rentals

Get 40% off when you reserve
for the whole month of June

Enjoy a writing residency surrounded by nature

Sohee checked their Instagram account. On the feed were photos of the meandering ridges, the guest rooms that resembled a writer's studio, a glasshouse garden filled with flowers, a walking path along the lake flanked by cherry blossoms in full bloom. It looked like a brand-new place that had opened less than two months ago. She quickly searched for blog reviews. Mostly positive. Without hesitation, she tapped on the 'Make a Reservation' button.

***

The writing studio on the first floor was cosier than she'd expected. It was the size of a living room in an average apartment. In the centre was a solid wooden table that could easily fit six. With white tones and simple décor, the space didn't feel stuffy at all. In fact, it was a perfect writing studio. In front of the window was a small tea table with a black electric kettle and a manual coffee grinder, next to three small potted plants. The built-in bookcase housed more than a hundred books, and in each section there were curated reads, ranging from novels to books about the arts.

A jazz piano rendition of 'Over the Rainbow' filtered from the white Bluetooth speaker on the shelf. A song from the movie *The Wizard of Oz*. Spotting a copy of the book hidden in a corner among its taller neighbours, her eyes lit up, as if seeing an old friend. She smiled.

It was her favourite book when she was a kid. Swept up in a hurricane, Dorothy finds herself in the Land of Oz. She asks for directions back home only to be told that no one but the all-knowing Wizard of Oz can help her. On the journey to meet him, she befriends the Scarecrow who wants a brain, the Tin Man who yearns to have a heart, and the Cowardly Lion seeking courage. After a series of adventures, they successfully meet the Wizard of Oz, but they are surprised and disappointed when he turns out to be an ordinary, short old man.

Sohee's favourite part was the twist – the realisation that the Scarecrow, Tin Man and Cowardly Lion had overcome their complexes through their adventures in search of the Wizard. Dorothy's belated realisation that her shoes had the magic power to return home also made an impression on Sohee.

She had a favourite line in the story, so much so that she wanted to inscribe it in her diary.

'You have plenty of courage, I am sure,' answered Oz.
'All you need is confidence in yourself. There is no
living thing that is not afraid when it faces danger.
The true courage is in facing danger when you are
afraid, and that kind of courage you have in plenty.'

Sohee looked out the window. The branches of the plum
blossoms swayed gently in the wind. She fell into deep
thought. These trees might not be able to uproot themselves
to go on adventures, but they stood strong and sturdy, looking
deep within themselves and growing wiser with age. It was as
if they were looking down at their silver shoes.

Behind her, the staff were giving her the introductory tour.

'. . . So feel free to read the books here. You can also bring
the books to the café; it's open until midnight. But please turn
off the lights if you're the last person. We also run a writers'
studio programme with two slots – 9 a.m. to 12 noon, and 2
p.m. to 5 p.m. You can either do your own writing or read.
Basically, it's to help people focus by setting aside a block of
time. If you drop by the café, I can give you more details.'

The staff member's voice was easy on the ears. Sohee
glanced at him. Handsomely tall with thick eyebrows and a
good fashion sense. But he looked a little nervous. He held a
palm-sized pad crammed with notes, and with his hand curled
over it, as if he were rolling a kimbap, he spoke like an actor
rehearsing his lines.

'To try and be more eco-friendly, we don't wash the towels
and the bedding every day, so we'll give you a new set every
four days. But if you need more in the meantime, please let
us know. Books from the café can also be read in your room.
The Wi-Fi details are in the brochure.'

'. . . Got it.'

She liked the place. Quite a bit, in fact. She kept all her praises inside, letting her expression remain blank. Also, she was simply too tired to talk. Not knowing what was going on in her mind, Siwoo looked at the Soyangri Book Kitchen's first long-term guest, uncertain of her muted reaction to the room.

It had been two months since Soyangri Book Kitchen opened its doors. The bulk of their customers were here for the café, and for the guests who booked a stay, it was usually for a quick getaway. This was the first time a guest was staying for the whole month. Siwoo had been nervous all morning. He was used to people singing their heartfelt praises about the book kitchen, saying that everything had exceeded their expectations. Many of them would snap photos and videos and upload them on their social media, without being prompted. Siwoo, who was naturally outgoing, often approached the guests to test a new coffee blend or to give feedback on a dessert he was perfecting. Usually, it wouldn't even take a day for him to get chummy with everyone.

But Ms Choi Sohee was the exception. She kept a poker face at all times. It wasn't like every guest would gush over their premises, but once they stared out the window, it was impossible not to be in awe of the landscape. But not Ms Choi. Siwoo had never encountered a guest who was more difficult to read. Even now, as Siwoo spoke, he couldn't help but wonder if he'd made a mistake.

'. . . Should you need anything else, please look for one of us at the café or call the number at the bottom right of the guide. Breakfast is at eight in the café. If you don't need breakfast, we'd appreciate it if you let us know in advance.'

Sohee gave a faint smile and nodded. Siwoo scratched his head, feeling self-conscious as he walked out. Sohee sat down at the chair facing the window. The hard wooden back was a stark contrast to the soft sofa in her office.

Next to the table was a dark green suitcase. The warm sunshine streaming in through the windows was calming. On the wall, the minute hand on the analogue clock crawled as if unaffected by the fast-paced life in Seocho-dong. The song 'Over the Rainbow' was ending. In her heart, she sang the last few lines.

Would her worries really melt like lemon drops here? What if every sweet promise turned out to be empty like in the *Wizard of Oz*? Without opening her suitcase, she closed her eyes and drifted off to sleep.

***

'It's been two weeks, and I still can't tell what she's thinking.'

'Who?'

'Our month-long guest – Choi Sohee.'

'Ms Choi? I liked her the moment I saw her,' said Yoojin as she watched Siwoo step into the café with a doubtful look on his face. 'Even if she keeps to herself all the time, she gives me the impression that she's someone with inner strength. Hyungjun, what do you think?'

'Seems like the calm, logical type. Maybe she's a graduate student writing her thesis, or a scriptwriter coming here to finish a project,' Hyungjun replied slowly as he recalled his impression of the quiet guest. Her long beige skirt and a thin white cardigan fitted her overall aura well.

At the book kitchen, Hyungjun was responsible for housekeeping and breakfast service. Whenever he went in to change the sheets and the towels, a jazz song would always be flowing in the background. Eddie Higgins Trio, Bill Evans, Stacey Kent,

Diana Panton – all Hyungjun's favourites. While he couldn't guess her job or her age, from her music taste, he was sure that she was a gentle, mild-mannered person.

'She hasn't skipped a single morning session at the writers' studio – maybe she's really an author?' Yoojin half-murmured to herself as she stuck the introduction cards for the new arrivals on the bookshelves. Meanwhile, Siwoo was organising the inventory, putting four books at once into the boxes as he spoke.

'It's been two weeks already. Like . . . How should I put it? It's like she has this protective membrane around her, you know the kind in superhero movies which gets activated when the villain attacks?'

Siwoo pretended to shoot sparks with finger guns when suddenly, a loud crack of thunder split the air. The couple sitting by the large window jumped. The next moment, rain pelted against the glass as grey clouds blanketed the sky. It was 2.37 p.m., yet it felt like nightfall already.

'It's as if the heavens were keeping it in the whole week just for the rain to fall on the weekend,' Yoojin grumbled.

Hyungjun, who was tabulating the inventory of the toiletries, looked up with worried eyes. The air indoors clumped in heavy silence. 'Rain's not the issue. I hope it doesn't escalate into a typhoon.'

Siwoo stacked up the boxes in the corner and fishing out his phone, he turned to Yoojin. 'It says a typhoon is moving from Japan and making its way through the ocean to Korea. Looks like it might become bigger when it makes landfall. Nuna, are you sure you still want to head out?'

Yoojin bit down on her lip. 'Of course! I've been looking forward to it for the longest time.'

She quickly checked the jazz festival's website. There was

only a pop-up notice on the safety guidelines. Luckily, there wasn't any announcement about cancelling the festival.

'Phew. Looks like they're going ahead. It's Stacey Kent's first time in Korea! And it's a stage collaboration with Little Flower!'

This was the fifth year of the Soyangri Jazz Music Festival. To spur regional tourism, the local government had gone all out with their support. Thanks to that, the star-studded line-up included Korea's key indie bands and about thirty top-rated domestic and international artists. It had grown to be a major jazz festival in Korea. When Yoojin found out that her favourite singer Stacey Kent was coming, she'd immediately bought a ticket. That was a month ago and today, the singer was set to perform at the primetime slot at seven in the evening.

Remembering that Hyungjun also enjoyed jazz, Siwoo turned to him instead. 'Don't tell me you're going, too? Did you leave behind your common sense?'

Outside, the strong winds were howling. Even the raindrops were sideswept and falling at an oblique angle. Hyungjun listened to the sharp whoosh tearing through the trees.

'. . . Doesn't seem like it'll escalate to a typhoon. But the rain's gonna be heavy.'

'You can tell just by listening to the rain? As expected of a Soyangri native.'

Hyungjun shot him an exasperated glance. 'The national weather service provides live updates on typhoons, just so you know.'

But it was also true that he grew up in tune with the sounds of the rain and wind. He couldn't exactly explain why, but he knew that the weather forecast was right, that the strong gusts would taper but it would rain the whole night. Just then his phone buzzed. It was an alert notification about the torrential rains in the region.

Yoojin and Hyungjun headed out at about four in the afternoon. The winds were still howling, like a tragic scene in an opera, and the branches swayed precariously. *Hopefully nothing happens,* Yoojin prayed in her heart. *What if there's a landslide or if the lake floods? Or if some bands got stuck on the way?*

***

Yoojin tilted her head. Where had she seen that person before? She looked like someone from her past, yet only a vague recollection remained. The memory was tickling her mind. It was only when she turned, for the third time, to stare that it hit her. The woman in a raincoat who was screaming and waving the light stick and bobbing to the music was their month-long guest Choi Sohee.

On stage, Stacey Kent had just introduced her new song and when she belted out the first note, Sohee was unrecognisable from her usual quiet self. The rain showed no signs of letting up. In fact, it was getting heavier. It was humid, but that didn't stop the audience from enjoying the performances in their raincoats. Those who came had braved the rain and there was this sense of heightened excitement, knowing that everyone must be ardent fans, given they'd gone the extra mile to be here. Sohee, too, rocked to the music as she sang along and clapped.

The performances ended slightly past nine. The rain was coming down harder and with the howling winds, and out of concern for the spectators, the artists had wanted to skip the encore, but of course, the audience was not having it. It was only after three encores that everyone exhaled in satisfaction, mixed with the lingering regret that the performance really was over, before delivering a loud and enthusiastic last cheer for the artists. As everyone shuffled to gather their belongings, the announcement over the speakers rang out to guide everyone to leave the venue safely.

'Sohee-ssi!'

Yoojin waited by the side for Sohee to get closer before calling out to her. Looking alarmed, she glanced around her, and spotting Yoojin, she smiled shyly.

'Yoojin Sajangnim! You came for the festival, too?'

Sohee glanced back at the throng of crowds leaving before walking towards Yoojin and Hyungjun. Water droplets were dripping from her raincoat cap. Despite the anorak, her face and her boots were soaked. The smell of sweat lingered in the air. Sohee's cheeks were flushed, and her eyes sparkled. Yoojin had never seen her so lively. At that thought, she smiled. 'You're into jazz?'

'Yeah. Not that I know much. But Murakami's novels talk a lot about jazz, and I got curious whether the music is like how he'd described it. I started listening and gradually found songs I enjoy. Just a casual fan. All thanks to Murakami, I'd say!'

Sohee looked at them in turn. 'How about you?'

Yoojin looked down at Sohee's soaked footwear and smiled. 'Yeah. Kind of similar to you, actually. Classical music is not quite my style, K-pop is a little too upbeat, indie music can be hard to understand . . . but jazz is easy on the ears. I like cool jazz in particular; I'll just let it play in the background while I read. It's more like I'm used to listening to it, not sure if I can say I *love* it.' Yoojin lightly jabbed Hyungjun. 'But Hyungjun here majored in music. He's in a completely different league from an amateur like me.'

'Wow, really?' Sohee's eyes sparkled with curiosity.

Flustered, Hyungjun immediately shook his head. 'No way. I'm a complete novice. I've returned everything to the profs.'

The three of them chuckled. It was as if something was connecting them in that moment; on most days, they were like separate islands with their own lives, but somewhere deep within the ocean, their feelings were connected by a similar melody.

Yoojin and Hyungjun had brought big umbrellas, but since they were soaked to their skin, they didn't bother opening them. They wouldn't be any use when the wind was blowing the rain sideways. With the heat of the performances still coursing through their blood, they didn't feel cold at all.

'We're going back to make hotcakes, would you like to join us? They're perfect for supper. We knew we'd get hungry, so we got everything prepared beforehand.'

***

The hotcakes were cooked to a perfect golden brown. From the freezer behind the counter, Hyungjun took out a tub of vanilla ice-cream. The downpour continued outside, occasionally crackling like a bonfire, or the rhythmic slosh of waves. Over the warm hotcakes and ice-cream, the three of them continued reliving the festival.

Yoojin was telling them how she became a fan of Stacey Kent.

'. . . Maybe that's why when she was singing "Postcard Lovers" just now, it was as if I was transported back to that trip with my friends – I could almost feel that day's wind, laughter, the warmth; all the memories came flooding back again . . .'

Next to Yoojin, Sohee was nodding.

'I know what you mean. Her voice makes me feel as though something in me is stirring, like I've become a goldfish swimming calmly in the tank. All is quiet, but I'm wrapped in a mix of loneliness, fear. And as the melody flows, it slowly soothes the mess of emotions in me.'

Something in the sounds of rain evoked old memories. Outside, the wind had tamed. For a while, there was silence around the table.

'You said you majored in music. How did you end up working here?' Sohee asked carefully.

A gust of wind whooshed in reply. Hyungjun looked a little awkward and when he spoke, Yoojin thought his low voice was like a cello.

'Yeah, I studied Applied Music. My dream was to become a lyricist. But nobody would hire an unknown name. I submitted actively to competitions, wrote proposals, did my best to boost my résumé, but it was no use. Two years passed, and I decided to give everything up and return to Soyangri. I was working part-time at a plant shop. The owner is my mum's close friend. There wasn't anything I wanted to do, or anything I knew that I could do. One day, I happened to pass by and saw the hiring notice at Soyangri Book Kitchen. I spent the entire night typing out my CV and cover letter.'

Yoojin grinned, as if thinking back to that day.

'During the interview, he was shaking so badly that he didn't quite make sense. But I liked the look in his eyes. There was sincerity within the desperation . . .'

In his cover letter, Hyungjun had outlined his vision for the Book Kitchen to be a space for words and stories, a place to rejuvenate and heal. He also came up with many ideas for programmes and activities, alongside a creative social media marketing plan. Even before the interview, Siwoo and Yoojin had already decided he was the one they were looking for. As the interview came to a close, Hyungjun's back was hunched with anxiety. Yoojin smiled at him.

'Can you start work next Monday? Construction is ongoing, so for a while, it may feel like you're working at a building site.'

There was something in the balmy wet weather. Something magical. As if time was drawing deep secrets from the well of one's heart. Feelings hiding from the sun would reveal themselves as the downpours started in the evenings. As if no matter what was said, the rain would wash it all away. And the well in her heart was threatening to overflow if she didn't let it out.

For a while, Sohee sat quietly, listening to the hum of the rain. Then she spoke.

'I went for a medical check-up . . . The doctor said it might be thyroid cancer. They found a tumour. High chance it's cancerous. They told me I should get it removed as soon as possible, so we've scheduled the surgery next month.'

The air stilled. Yoojin whipped her head around and stared disbelievingly at Sohee. Hyungjun's expression froze on his face. Outside, the breeze had died, making the silence even more pronounced. Even the rain seemed to read the tension in the room. Sohee, however, looked calm, as though she was recounting someone else's story.

'The doctor said it was lucky that we discovered it early, so once the tumour is removed, I should be able to go on with life as usual, 90 per cent full recovery rate – that's what they said. Anyway, medical technology is so advanced these days. Nothing to worry about, I suppose.'

Sohee paused to pierce a small piece of the leftover hotcake with her fork. The scent of vanilla ice-cream tickled her nose.

'My youngest uncle died from thyroid cancer about ten years ago. We weren't particularly close . . . but that was the first time someone around me passed away. I was probably twenty years old then, but I still remember it to this day. All of us will die, but that was my first time witnessing death. Uncle was gone too early – he was only in his early fifties. Back then, the loss of life seemed like such a huge event. But now, ten years on, being told I have cancer . . . Well, if you ask me what's on my mind . . .'

Sohee paused, as though trying to organise her thoughts. Outside, the torrential rain showed no signs of easing. Yoojin and Hyungjun sat quietly, like theatre actors who knew it wasn't their turn to speak. They nodded encouragingly.

Sohee exhaled, expelling a small sigh.

'. . . *Did ten years just flash by like this?* That was my first thought. I was twenty when Uncle passed away. Now I'm thirty-two. At this rate, in the blink of an eye, I'll be fifty soon.'

Yoojin sipped her cold coffee as Hyungjun stared ahead, locked in his own thoughts. The slight tremor in Sohee's voice belied her calm expression. Raising a slender finger, she brushed back a lock of hair on her forehead before releasing her ponytail and retying it, as if that would help her gather herself again.

'The perfect moment in life doesn't exist,' said Sohee after a pause. 'The fact is that we are constantly in a state of imperfection, and when the time comes, the curtains will close on our stage. But when I was younger, I wasn't thinking about life and death at all. I was good at exams; I breezed through the Korean education system. I have a competitive streak, and I'm particularly good at closed-ended questions with a definite answer. Naturally, I got accepted into a good university. Later, I aced law school, got a job immediately and ever since then, work has become my life.'

Sohee glanced out the window as memories of the years in school and at work flashed through her mind. She took a deep breath, inhaling the smell of the rain, her gaze falling somewhere in the far distance. As she picked up the coffee mug, she raised the other hand to her hair, as if to check if her ponytail was still holding up well.

'I was just staring at the medical report, the suspected diagnosis, the doctor's recommendation to run more tests when suddenly, a thought crossed my mind. Could this . . . be a letter from Uncle? I imagined him writing from heaven. *Sohee-ya. Think about what you really want in life, not what others tell you is good for you. Life's shorter than you think.*'

Yoojin was reminded of the day Sohee first arrived at Soyangri Book Kitchen. She looked spent, as if her soul was elsewhere. Her dark green suitcase was huge, but Yoojin suspected, from the way it clattered loudly when she dragged it across the uneven ground, that it was almost empty. Summer had arrived and the lush greenery seemed to be celebrating the prime of life, but Yoojin couldn't detect a single bit of vitality in Sohee. She looked lonely, as though she'd crash-landed on a deserted star.

But tonight, with the rain forming a film of water on the windowpanes, she looked much more at ease. Yoojin thought she could detect a faint glow, just a glimmer, on Sohee's face. But she didn't say anything. As she listened to Sohee, it felt as though her own life story was also being read out.

Sohee took a long sip of her coffee and continued.

'Perhaps I've been hiding in my safe zone all this time. Everyone says I've got my life sorted out early, that I'm set to cruise along the expressway. They applaud me for passing notoriously difficult exams and maintaining a strong lead in the rat race. Honestly, I've never once paused to reflect if this is even the game I want to play. Is this who I hoped to be? I threw myself to it, but I've never wondered what's at the end of the road.'

How do you want to live your life? Nobody ever asked Sohee that. So what if she was the top student? Never once had anyone spoken to her about her interests, or what she really wanted to do in life. Back then, she hadn't felt the urgency to delve into those questions, so she simply made it her goal to stay ahead in the competition that surrounded her. And for the longest time, that was how she'd been living.

'The medical report put a hard stop to everything. As if it's staring right at me, asking: *Do you know what you really want? Do you know yourself?*'

Nodding, Yoojin looked at Sohee. 'Perhaps . . . it's not such a bad thing.'

'What is?'

'That you're being forced to take a break. That you won't keep moving forward blindly and suddenly find yourself on the last page of your life. That you're given a chance to pause and think.'

'Hmm, that's true . . .'

There was a moment of silence.

'There's this book by Kim Youngmin – *Morning Is the Time to Think about Death*,' Yoojin said as she tapped absent-mindedly against her mug. Outside, the thunder rumbled. *Kung kung.* For a split second, it felt as though the ground was opening to swallow her up.

'My friend was the one who recommended it to me, and she was gushing over how it's full of wisdom. I remember the author quoting Mike Tyson – *Everybody has a plan until they get punched in the face.*'

They laughed. The tension in the air seemed to ease. There was a pause as Yoojin lifted the coffee mug to her lips and drank a mouthful.

'The book questions many of the so-called norms or life's milestones – like marriage, education, success – and why we're so obsessed. The book goes on to talk about how life is too short and too precious to read things that bore us, to listen to long, meaningless speeches. I like how it's telling us to reflect on our life, do what excites us.'

Sohee nodded slowly. Yoojin gazed steadily at her.

'So what I'm saying is . . . this might be an opportunity. It's not that life has screeched to a halt; you're being given a gift – to figure out what matters and live the life you truly want.'

'I suppose . . .' Sohee murmured as she wrapped her hands around her mug. 'A chance card.'

Hyungjun, who'd been listening quietly, nodded. 'My chance card was an air ticket to Australia. After serving in the army, I did a working holiday there.'

This was the first time Yoojin had heard about it.

'Wait, you did?'

'Yeah . . .'

Hyungjun glanced down at his lukewarm coffee, his deep voice in harmony with the rain. Tonight, something was stirring on his usually stoic face.

'Or rather, I escaped to Australia. I was supposed to finish up my studies. But it's not like I had any plans after graduating from the Applied Music department. Then one day, my house-mate was commenting about how we can't see the North Star in the southern hemisphere. And that in Australia, the moon moves in a different direction across the sky.'

As if finding it awkward to hear his own voice, Hyungjun paused to clear his throat. What time is it now? Yoojin wondered, but for some reason, she couldn't find her bearings. Instead, her thoughts drifted to Hyungjun picking tomatoes in the never-ending stretch of fields, the full moon tracing its path across the sky while he and his roommate were fast asleep.

Hyungjun continued. 'In the northern hemisphere, the North Star is fixed in the sky. And people use it as a landmark – an unchanging standard, so to speak. But below the equator, things are different. I remember gazing up at the night sky of Brisbane and thinking . . . if we are lost in the inky darkness of the desert, won't looking at different stars tell us a different direction? Imagine being on a snow-capped mountain, surrounded by a blanket of white. I suppose if you're in the northern hemisphere, you'll try to find the North Star, but those below the equator will have to seek out the dimmer South Star. Even something simple like donuts mean different things to different people. While some may insist that donuts have a hole in the middle, that's not true of the earliest donuts. What I'm trying to say is . . . life need not follow a single trajectory.'

Yoojin thought of a novel she'd read. Set in a world where there are two moons, people are used to seeing twin orbs in the night sky. Not the protagonist, who hails from a different world. When everyone eyes him suspiciously for questioning the 'norm', he becomes flustered. There's only one moon in his world; how can he suddenly accept that there are two? But in this world, he's the odd one out for doubting something that has already been proven scientifically.

Sohee nodded. 'I get it. It's like how our society glorifies achievements like the "youngest so-and-so", "the first one to achieve something". We forget that everyone blooms differently; there are such diverse paths in life. It's like we've become conditioned to feel anxious should we stray the slightest from the norm. What are we? The GPS system?'

Her voice was calm, like the winter rain falling silently over a brook at daybreak. Instead of anger, there was a tinge of despair.

Yoojin nodded. 'Society never stops reminding us that a successful life is to stand at the top of the pyramid. We aren't allowed to fall, even if we're still learning how to walk . . . We grow up with a deep-set fear that the moment we deviate from the path, we're going to fall off the cliff.'

Hyungjun let out a bitter laugh.

'Right? Even the GPS doesn't automatically recommend the shortest route . . .'

'Exactly! Such a simple logic, why don't people get it? We should be seeking the optimal route!'

Everyone nodded appreciatively. *Optimal route* – Sohee felt a ripple in her heart. *Life isn't a hundred-metre sprint, it isn't quite a marathon either. Perhaps life is simply the journey of finding our own pace and direction – the optimal path for ourselves.*

'Oh, I've been wanting to ask,' said Hyungjun, meeting Sohee's gaze. His voice was no longer awkward. 'What had you planned to do when you booked the stay?'

'My plan? To have no plans. I just want to spend some time close to nature, maybe do some reading and keep a diary. Oh yes. And go to the jazz festival!'

They laughed. The air around them felt smooth and soft, like a well-kneaded dough.

Hyungjun nodded. 'I remember seeing you deep in concentration over your notebook. So that's your diary?'

'Yeah. At first, I was just jotting down some thoughts. But I found myself thinking about the story of *The Wizard of Oz*, how the world appears green because everyone's wearing green-tinted spectacles. I start to wonder, so what does their world look like without those spectacles? I imagine there'll be different colours . . . and just like how each of us has a colour that fits us the best, won't the same apply to books too? I started writing a story about a magical bookshop that helps customers find the book of their life.'

Yoojin's eyes lit up.

'That sounds amazing. I'd love to read it.'

'It's very much a rough draft. Just rambling thoughts. If a story is a painting, mine is like a kid's doodles!'

Sohee felt as though her heart was not so empty anymore. As if by sharing her story, a weight that had been pressing down between her throat and her chest was slowly melting away.

In the pitch darkness, a faint light flickered. A part of herself that had sunk to the bottom of the lake was lifted again as she confided in Yoojin and Hyungjun. The pelting rain felt like an upbeat jazz rhythm that was drumming in support of her. A smile spread across her face. I'm so glad I came, she thought.

The summer monsoon might seem relentless, but Yoojin knew the storms would stop one day. Like how life was finite; after today, all of us were a step closer to the end. It was impossible to live life simply enduring our nights on earth. All of us needed time to let our hair down, time untouched by the typhoons.

Yoojin chewed a piece of hotcake, now cold, as she listened to their conversation. Sohee would become a judge in no time, she had no doubt. That would just be the start of her journey, not her destination. Yoojin rooted for her silently in her heart. She imagined that one day, Sohee would have a day job as a judge, writing stories at night. A few years down the road, maybe she'd walk into a bookshop and see Sohee's books on the shelves. Sohee would find her optimal route.

4

A MIDSUMMER NIGHT'S DREAM

After five hours on her feet, Serin finally had a moment to catch her breath. She sat down and watched from afar as the bride headed towards the wedding reception in her mini wedding gown. She looked a little tired, but hugely relieved that her outdoor wedding ceremony had ended well. Her fingers laced with her husband's as she greeted her family and guests with a bright smile.

For the past few weeks, the August sun had blazed down on Soyangri, but today, the sky was a light grey. The cloud cover, acting like tinted car windows, absorbed some of the heat. Clusters of hydrangeas, like bouquets of everlasting love, bloomed elegantly in the garden. The guests, who had travelled from afar, exchanged pleasant greetings, and someone commented that the weather wasn't as hot as they had expected.

The outdoor wedding was Serin's first project after joining Soyangri Book Kitchen last month. Or rather, it was a series of unplanned coincidences that brought her here. Ever since she went back to Seoul in April, she'd been gushing to everyone around her about how beautiful and charming the place was, as well as sharing photos and videos on her blog and Instagram. One day, she got a DM.

—Serin nuna, do you think it's possible to hold an outdoor wedding ceremony and reception at the book kitchen?

Jihoon? It took her several seconds before she remembered that he was a younger cousin of Namwoo oppa, her ex-boyfriend. Aha. That intelligent and warm-hearted boy who was living in Germany. Serin recalled how despite having lived in Berlin for more than twenty years, he didn't have the vibes of the stereotypical overseas Korean.

Serin replied immediately.

—Of course! I'm sure the bride will love it! I can imagine it would be so romantic, like a glasshouse wedding. But omg, are you getting married?

—If only, ha! Not me. A senior colleague in my research lab. The bride-to-be wants an outdoor wedding or the ceremony in a glasshouse. But the good venues in Seoul are fully booked, so the couple are looking elsewhere.

—My friend works there. I'll ask him!

Serin had immediately dropped Siwoo a text.

As luck would have it, she ended up planning the wedding and joining the Soyangri Book Kitchen team. Officially, she oversaw the merchandise design and the marketing plans, but unofficially, she also handled outdoor weddings, receptions, seminars, and other small-scale events.

If sitting in front of the computer and working on illustrations was akin to a hundred-metre sprint, planning an outdoor wedding was a full marathon. From the wedding reception buffet, the décor, to the music, the hustling never seemed to end. Over the last few weeks, she'd recced the outdoor wedding venues at famous hotels for inspiration, and met up with different caterers for food tasting. To find the most suitable lighting and décor, she'd visited several places. In some sense, it wasn't that different from her previous work; Soyangri Book Kitchen was like a huge canvas where she could design the dream wedding.

'Nuna! It's been forever!'

'Jihoon! You've become quite the ajusshi, huh?' Serin teased.

It had been four years since they last met, but there was none of the awkwardness. Jihoon reminded her of her first love, Namwoo oppa. He wasn't exactly the talkative type, but she found it easy to talk to him. The last time they met, he'd just completed his mandatory military service, sporting a crew cut, his skin rough with a smattering of pimples. But today, Jihoon was suave. Decked out in a dark navy suit, his shoulders had become broader, and his longish hair styled nicely with wax. The polished black leather shoes went well with his suit, which he paired with grey and dark purple striped socks that added a pop of colour. He smiled, and she thought he looked a lot more at ease, softer around the edges. Somewhat more polished, too.

'When you contacted me, I thought you were the one getting married. How did you end up in research? Are you now based in Korea?'

'I'm doing my master's degree in psychology here. I applied four years ago, after completing military service. I plan to root myself in Korea – if that's the right way of putting it.'

He grinned, and his eyes arched into familiar crescents. *When Namwoo oppa smiles, he looks just like this . . .* These days, thinking of him no longer felt like a knife twisting in her guts. The emotions had blunted. Sometimes she could even recall the good old times with a fuzzy feeling in her chest.

'Guess there's no place like Korea. Anyway, that lady over there . . . is that the friend?' Serin lowered her voice to a whisper.

Jihoon nodded and smiled, but a shadow flashed past his eyes. He let out a short sigh, as though trying to suppress his nervousness.

'. . . Mm yeah. That's the friend I told you about. Mari.'

***

Mari and Jihoon had known each other for a long time. She'd moved to Berlin with her father and older sister when she was around two, while Jihoon relocated with his family when he was six. However, they grew up in completely different environments.

Mari's father operated a business in the arms trade. Or at least that was what she grew up knowing. Her father's life was shrouded in mystery, and she could never read his thoughts. *Mother* was a taboo word in their family.

Because she had no other relatives in Berlin, there was no one she could ask about her mum. Instead, she spent her time imagining the kind of clothes that would've suited her, the expressions she made when taking photos. Many a time, Mari stood in front of the mirror, examining her features carefully and wondering which parts of her she'd inherited.

Unlike Mari and her father, whose relationship seemed to be bound only by blood ties, Jihoon's family was the definition of warmth; they would confide in one another about their happiness and worries.

Jihoon's parents ran a launderette in Berlin's Korea Town, working long hours each day, where they started before sunrise and only closed at 11 p.m. His mother wore a perpetually tired look with puffy permed hair, and in his memory, his father was always worried about not having enough money to tide them over for the month. Yet Jihoon never grew up feeling like he didn't have enough.

No matter how busy they were, never once would his parents skip a day of looking into his eyes and telling him how much they loved him. They kept a special coin bank at home where his parents would drop in a coin or note every now and then, saving up over the entire year to buy him a birthday present. On their only rest day of the week, Sunday, they'd bring him to explore Berlin's sights – parks, galleries, the museum of natural history, the zoo. The photos that captured these shared moments were abundant evidence of warmth and love in their close family. In Jihoon's memories, his parents were always positive, doing the best they could. Over the years, he realised that it was actually the best life lesson his parents could've taught him. He grew up a well-loved and secure child.

Life started to get better in their fifth year living in Berlin. The launderette had a steady business, and with their earnings, they bought out the grocer next door. Not long after, they opened a second launderette in Mitte, Berlin's central borough, and despite raising their fees, they continued to get a steady stream of customers through word-of-mouth recommendations. The customers who came stayed for the genuine service. The launderette felt warm and cosy, and there was always a bright smile greeting them at the grocer. What kept the customers coming back wasn't because they *had* to wash their clothes, or that they were hungry. It was the warmth and sincerity which greeted them when they entered, his parents' ability to smooth the creases in their feelings, that filled their hearts.

When he was eleven, his parents transferred him to an international school about a thirty-minute car ride away. It was a dream come true for them. The international school boasted a top-notch curriculum and the best educational environment. While the tuition fees set them back tens of million won a year, never once did they feel the pinch.

When he started school, Jihoon was nervous. The elegant red-brick building displayed its tradition and heritage, and inside, he was greeted by a stylish, modern interior. The class was kept small, about fifteen students, and all subjects were taught in English.

The students enjoyed a wide variety of activities on campus, including horseback riding, swimming, tennis, soccer, flute, ballet and theatre. Their form teacher was kind. Jihoon marvelled at the infrastructure – the high vaulted, elegant ceilings, the sports field where the grass was always well kept. He quickly made new friends from all over the world and settled down well in the school.

On his first day, Jihoon immediately recognised the girl who was sitting in the second row in class. Or rather, a memory in the recesses of his mind sprung up and flashed before his eyes – the first time he had met Mari. He was eight back then. At Berlin's Museum of Natural History, she had been sitting on a bench at the central hall, completely expressionless, next to her older sister, who wore a solemn look. He had walked past her, but something about her made him turn back. She was as pretty as a wax doll, but in her eyes was a shadow that didn't seem to fit her age.

Jihoon had then realised that the girl was also staring at him. Staring at his parents who were smiling brightly and holding his hand on both sides. His mum was chattering away in Korean, and until they passed through the arched doorway to the next room of taxidermised butterflies and insects, he had felt the girl's stare on his back. When their gazes met, an inexplicable something was etched in his heart forever.

***

Mari, now twenty-eight, would never allow herself to get drunk. Even when everyone was egging each other on at drinking parties, she'd pretend to be drunk. Everyone had believed that she couldn't hold her alcohol, but that wasn't true. Mari also didn't believe in hypnosis or therapy. Or rather, she avoided them at all costs. The possibility that she'd let slip her innermost thoughts was frightening. Before speaking, she always made sure that the lies would add up. She hated to risk a crack in her perfect pretence . . . Before she realised it, lying had become her default mode. It made her more comfortable. The truth, on the other hand, was always hard.

At the wedding, a man came up to Mari.

'Won't you miss it here when you go back to the States?'

'I will, but my mum is eager to have me back,' she replied.

Mari had returned to Korea on a year's placement, and was working in the same research lab as Jihoon. Thinking that her answer would be sufficient to end the conversation with her colleague, she turned away to take in the surroundings. As the sun set, the garden where the wedding ceremony had taken place transformed into the reception venue. Lights lined the path like stepping stones and waltz music fitting for the summer evening played from a speaker somewhere.

Of course, there wasn't a mother who was waiting for her in the States. But the more she spoke about her mum, her existence sharpened in her mind. Her affectionate mum who loved to pout cutely. Like the finest scriptwriter who makes her characters come to life, Mari was also writing her life's script. She had all the little details memorised and to her, everything was real, as if she'd cast a magic spell. It was easy, especially when she had a reference – Jihoon's mother. It made her script come alive.

As she carefully crafted her lies, the fictional world blended with real life. Nobody ever suspected anything. In any case, wasn't life a mix of truth and lies? In the falsehoods lay a beautiful and comforting world she'd built for herself.

'Would be nice if she could join you here in Korea . . . It's quite hard to produce substantial research if you're only here for a one-year exchange programme. Maybe you should . . .'

Was he terrible at reading the room, or was it just his way of being friendly? The colleague continued to engage her in conversation as he swirled the champagne in his flute glass. He was working on his PhD, researching cognitive psychology in the field of media communication.

Mari watched the bubbles sparkle in his glass. 'Ah, please excuse me.'

Flashing a smile that showed off her even teeth, Mari gently but firmly put an end to the conversation. Gazing past him, she nodded as if greeting someone else. The guy turned, but he couldn't tell who she'd seen. All around were colleagues and seniors from the research lab, chatting and laughing.

Like a chameleon, Mari effortlessly blended in with the crowd. She smiled, thinking back to the night she'd gone with her colleagues to the noraebang for karaoke, the way they'd scream-sung and shouted, their arms wrapped around each other's shoulders in comradeship as they clinked glasses. She enjoyed the boisterous mood of Korean drinking parties. Having grown up overseas, in Germany and the United States, the community spirit of Korean culture was new to her. For the first time in a long while, Mari felt a sense of calm, as if she'd returned home.

The buffet table boasted a delectable spread of Korean dishes. There were pork galbi ribs, japchae – sweet potato starch noodles stir fried with vegetables – as well as all kinds of savoury pancakes, kimbap, chobap, bulgogi, banquet noodles and more. The ceramic tableware had a simple design, yet exuded elegance. Mari thought back to Christmas dinners at Jihoon's house. Jihoon's mum came from Yeosu in the South Jeolla Province, and during Christmastime, she tried to recreate the taste of her hometown in Berlin. And always, she was successful. It was a major affair. Where possible, she flew in the ingredients from Korea, and sourced the rest locally. The highlights were the gat kimchi made with mustard greens, braised mackerel with aged kimchi, spicy seafood stew, and a glorious spread of more than nine banchan – side dishes – braised eggs in soy sauce, seasoned beansprouts, pan-fried tofu. The spread took up the entire table.

It was the first time that Mari had tried Korean food which focused on seafood. She was familiar with bulgogi and non-spicy kimchi, but never had she eaten spicy seafood stew, spicy braised fish, mustard greens kimchi instead of the ones made from napa cabbage. But the moment she put the food into her mouth, it was as if her tastebuds had craved it for the longest time, and the flavours melted in her soul.

Her Korean wasn't perfect, but she could understand almost everything Jihoon and his mum said. When she was with his family, she didn't have to make up any stories. They were average in every way, yet they believed that if they lived on their own terms, they could shine in life. The idea of basking in a sense of superiority, even if it meant living beyond their means, never occurred to them. They were always down to earth, and never once had they attempted to show off, like 'Oh I've done it before, so I know . . .' or 'I've earned big bucks . . .' or to be a pretentious know-it-all, saying things like 'In life, who doesn't have that kind of experience?'

When she was hanging out with Jihoon and his family, Mari was freed from the pressure of needing to be perfect or unique. Neither Jihoon nor his parents had ever tried to probe into her private life or her family. They didn't give her the curious look, or ask her in a roundabout way what kind of job her father did, whether she was well off. Neither did they initiate uncomfortable small talk like what was the most significant memory she had with her mum, or her dreams for the future. To his parents, Mari was simply Jihoon's friend, and to him, she was his friend, and also a link to his Korean roots. *That's enough, isn't it?* It was as if his eyes said that. In his company, she could always be herself.

'Hey, Mari! Here!'

Jihoon, who was at the other end of the garden, called out to her. His voice wasn't loud, but she turned immediately. As Mari weaved her way through the guests to him, several male colleagues at the research lab turned to glance at her.

Mari had a fair complexion, a perfectly shaped oval forehead and big eyes with defined double eyelids like a Barbie doll. Her hair, dyed to a light honey brown, was tied up in a ponytail that swayed in the wind as she walked. Her plain black dress wrapped around her model-like figure. She was only wearing light make-up, but it accentuated her striking features. While her shoulders were a tad slouched, like a scared kid, her steps were light and graceful like a ballerina. Mari gave off a mysterious aura; there was something unfamiliar about her.

'Hey hey, you haven't changed at all,' Jihoon teased as he reached out a hand to steady Mari, who had almost tripped. Mari looked up and took in his smart suit and friendly grin. Her gaze turned to the woman next to him, who looked like the cute, friendly type.

'How is it that you're still as clumsy?' he laughed.

***

Mari was always tripping over herself. Whether it was during ballet lessons back in school, along the corridors as they moved to a different class, during the Halloween party in the garden at the dorm, on the stage rehearsing for a musical. In fact, that was how they'd first got closer – because she'd tripped. That day, back in Berlin, they were almost going to collide in the corridor when at the last second, Mari swerved and tripped, twisting her ankle. Because she couldn't stand up, he'd had to piggyback her to the nurse's room. From then on, they became each other's shadow.

Mari had to keep her cast on for four weeks, and because Jihoon thought he was also responsible, he offered to carry her bag and belongings for her. They did their maths homework together, as well as their assigned readings, like *To Kill a Mockingbird*, *Anne of Green Gables* and *The Little Prince*.

Christmas that year, Mari met Jihoon's parents for the first time.

'Aigoo! How pretty!'

Jihoon's mum embraced Mari the moment she saw her, as if she was an aunt who hadn't seen her niece for a few years. Mari was flustered. Her expression froze on her face, but she didn't dislike the hug that smelt of delicious food and warmth.

Jihoon grinned. 'Mum, this is Mari, the friend I told you about. She's most comfortable using German, but she speaks Korean too. She has had a Korean tutor since kindergarten.'

'It's not easy to keep your native tongue in a foreign country. You've done us Koreans proud!'

Jihoon's dad was wearing a stiffly ironed suit. Mari carefully took his proffered hand and was a little surprised to find his handshake less formal than she'd expected.

For the next six years, Mari joined Jihoon's family for their annual Christmas dinner. Jihoon thought this tradition would continue, but on the seventh year, Mari vanished on Christmas Eve. Ten years passed, and he never saw Mari again. She seemed determined to wipe all traces of herself. In the passing years, there were more than enough opportunities for her to reach out, but she never did.

Jihoon graduated from Leipzig University with a degree in psychology. He'd believed that they would somehow reunite at university, and he tried his best to track down any clue that could lead to her, but there was nothing. She didn't keep in contact with anyone. She wasn't on social media. But he refused to give up. His heart wouldn't allow him to. The times they'd spent together, he'd thought it friendship, but with her gone, it was as if a part of him had vanished together with her. An aching sense of longing filled him, and their memories became crisper than the autumn foliage. Gradually, he realised that he thought of her as more than a friend.

As he ruminated on the times they had spent together, it suddenly became clear to him that when Mari was with others, she'd put on a mask and hide her true self. Back then, he hadn't thought much of it, but on reflection, Mari was more comfortable with the mask on. He deeply regretted how despite his vague realisation, he'd never asked her about it, or been around to listen to her.

Mari was complicated, cautious. There were many sides of her that he didn't understand, but he was sure he'd seen her true, raw self. The girl who was fearful, prone to cry secretly when alone, who craved being an average teenager . . .

And right now, he was watching Mari bask in the sunset glow in the garden of Soyangri Book Kitchen. Suppressing the tender feelings inside him, he introduced Serin to Mari.

'This is Serin nuna. A famous illustrator.'

'He likes to exaggerate. Haha. I heard you two were close friends when he was living in Germany?'

'Oh. Yeah. I'm . . .' Mari swallowed hard. 'I'm Mari.'

Mari wondered if she should just pretend to be bad at Korean and worm her way out of this situation. She couldn't quite put a finger on it, but looking at her childhood friend now decked out in a smart suit, next to a cute lady whose eyes arched into crescents when she beamed, was stressing her out. Was it because she knew she wouldn't be able to lie?

'Mari? What a beautiful name. It suits you. Oh right!' Serin exclaimed as if she had suddenly thought of something. She spoke calmly, but her excitement was palpable.

'We are running a nighttime event at our bookshop, starting at seven. Several indie bookshops are taking turns to have a special day where we open till late, and there's going to be a book club meeting too. It's our turn today, and since the wedding reception is expected to end by seven, we've decided to go ahead with our late-night bookshop. Our boss is going to host the book club. Since you're already here, would you like to join us?'

Serin held out a brochure. Jihoon smiled and nodded encouragingly at Mari. She took the paper, not noticing the meaningful look the other two exchanged. She read the introduction of the Midsummer Night Book Club.

August Pick: Where the Crawdads Sing *by Delia Owens*

Lend your ears to the voices of loneliness and solitude as we discuss the life of Kya, who was abandoned in the marshlands when she was a child.

Mari had no interest whatsoever about the life of an abandoned young girl. She recoiled from the brochure, keeping a cool expression on her face as she replied.

'It's fine. I'll just grab a café latte or—'

'Come on, Mari. Let's go together,' Jihoon urged. In his low voice was a hint of resolve. Unconsciously, Mari turned towards him and their eyes met.

His dark pupils were a clear lake: calm waters, reflecting warm shimmering moonlight. In her mind's eye, a young elephant languidly drank from the lakeshore, and a gentle wind blew in the silence. Even if the sun didn't reach this place, all was good. On the other hand, Mari's eyes contained a dizzy, chaotic world. A rollercoaster zoomed past, the screams of its riders scattering shattered pieces of memories. Their desolate landscape was dotted with dilapidated houses that looked like they might collapse at any moment.

Jihoon kept his gaze steady, as if telling her: *Mari, it's fine. Everything will be okay.*

In his eyes were feelings that ran too deep, too complex to be expressed by imperfect words. Mari was afraid. She felt as if she was becoming transparent under his gaze. Mari knew that her life was like wading in a deep pit of secrets. No way was she dragging him down with her. Without saying anything, she merely maintained eye contact. But she felt her resolve crumbling.

***

In the seminar room at the book café, readings were ongoing. Slow piano music flowed in the background. Six or seven people were seated at the long wooden table, their attention on the participant reading aloud in front of the projector.

> Months passed, winter easing gently into place, as southern winters do. The sun, warm as a blanket, wrapped Kya's shoulders, coaxing her deeper into the marsh. Sometimes she heard night-sounds she didn't know or jumped from lightning too close, but whenever she stumbled, it was the land that caught her. Until at last, at some unclaimed moment, the heart-pain seeped away like water into sand. Still there, but deep. Kya laid her hand upon the breathing, wet earth, and the marsh became her mother.

The sentences unrolled into sounds which vibrated in the air. Through the reader's voice, the printed word was delivered into the world like a newborn. The seminar room turned into Kya's marshlands. Calls of the cicadas could be heard in the distance, like grass rustling in the wind, and outside the window, a few fireflies glowed like stray shooting stars.

Yoojin, who was hosting the book club, spoke.

'I think everyone will relate to Kya, even if it's in different ways. When she was five, her mother walked out and never came back again. And her siblings, who'd had enough of their father's abuse, also moved out one by one, and in the end, her alcoholic father left her behind in the marshlands.'

Mari felt seen. As if the secrets she'd wrapped, again and again, now lay bare in the sun, melting away the protective mask that had been her second skin. Mari imagined herself looking into Kya's blue eyes.

'While the world's making up all kinds of rumours about Kya, she finds a friend in loneliness and grows up in the comfort of the marshlands,' Yoojin continued. 'Later, when Chase, who's captivated by Kya's beauty, and her childhood friend Tate appear in the story, her life undergoes a rapid wave of changes. Through the depictions of Kya's struggles with isolation and her relationship with Tate, the author explores the meaning of loneliness and love.'

When Jihoon read the novel two years ago, he had immediately thought of Mari. Back then, he'd thought that she would never reappear in his life ever again. He'd imagined her living somewhere under the vast blue sky and hoped that the book would somehow find its way to her.

Jihoon was sure that Mari would find peace in the marshlands of the story. That she'd be comforted on a deeper level than chatting with someone for hours at a café or bar. It would be as if Kya was sitting silently next to Mari as they watched the sunset together. She'd accompany Mari through the melancholy and loneliness as the sun coloured the sky a fiery red. If only Mari could read the book, she'd have a friend to confide in. She'd be able to tell Kya her story . . .

When the first session ended, the book club participants chatted softly as they got up for a break. Jihoon excused himself to go to the bathroom. Left alone, Mari reached out for the book on the table and started reading the first page. Within a few sentences, she was absorbed.

From behind, she heard Jihoon's voice.

'Are you ready?'

She turned around in surprise.

'Huh?'

Jihoon raised the mosquito repellent in his hand.

'A midsummer night's walk.'

Mari stared at him, mouth agape. 'Like right now? Can't you see that I'm wearing heels?'

Jihoon grinned. He could read the child-like excitement in her eyes.

From the backyard of Soyangri Book Kitchen, Jihoon turned on to a narrow walking path. The warm, humid air of midsummer lingered like a hot-air balloon which couldn't take off. There were no lights along the path, but because of the moonlight, the surroundings were bright, and there were several others on the nature trail. And the fireflies. In the summer night, several kids looking to be around seven or eight years old chased after them, laughing and shouting. The weather was humid, but the wind in the forest was cool, swirling gently like the dancing fireflies.

'If I knew I'd be hiking, I'd have changed into sneakers,' Mari grumbled.

'I knew you were going to say that.' Jihoon grinned. He set down his backpack and took out a pair of sneakers.

'Oh, wait. What . . .?'

'Your birthday present. EU 36.5, am I right?'

'Yeah . . .'

Jihoon placed the sneakers casually in front of her. After

a moment's hesitation, she slipped out of her heels and put them on.

'Did you know? In Korea, if you give someone shoes as a present, it means they'll run away from you.'

Jihoon gazed up into her eyes. Mari, who knew from his expression what he was about to say, felt her chest squeeze.

'You're already a pro at disappearing.'

Jihoon spoke lightly as if his comment was a joke, but underneath there was strong resentment in his heart. Not knowing how to respond, she remained silent. Jihoon helped her up and pointed ahead.

'That's the way down. It's about a five-minute walk and we'll reach a stretch of wetland.'

They turned on to a smaller fork in the road. Ahead was the small piece of wetland. Several couples were holding hands and admiring the scenery. The calls of bugs and frogs added to the cacophony of the cicadas; it was so loud that Mari could almost feel her eardrums pounding. A gust of cool wind blew. Occasionally, the mountain mosquitoes buzzed loudly in her ears. The sides of the sneakers were scraping her bare feet slightly, but she was happy. To be in Korea, walking next to Jihoon in the forest of fireflies in midsummer, felt unreal. Wait. She realised something strange. How did he know of this place when it was also his first time at Soyangri?

'Almost there.'

'Woah . . . What are these?'

'Indeed, what are these?'

Jihoon gave a soft laugh. On the ground was a red checked picnic mat, and in the open basket, he spotted dessert and a bottle of champagne. Leaning against the basket was a postcard with an illustration of fireflies in the forest. And a handwritten message – *To Jihoon and Mari.*

'Serin nuna – you met her just now – told me this is a great place to see fireflies. She was like, *Oh, if you go there, you'll see something.* Now I get what she meant, haha!'

Dozens of fireflies were flying across the puddle-like water, as if sending a message in secret code. As Mari sipped the champagne, she couldn't tear her eyes away from their glow.

'It's wonderful here. As if I've stepped into another universe.'

'This place didn't used to have fireflies. Soyangri Book Kitchen got them from Muju County.'

'Really? They've really put in the effort for this place.'

Mari looked around curiously. Jihoon smiled his signature soft smile as he nodded.

'If we follow the path we were on just now, we'll reach the lake. In the past, it used to be a busy road for the villagers. But when a new highway was built nearby, people no longer needed this road. So the Book Kitchen folks decided to come up with this firefly tour to show off how beautiful this place is.'

A faint smile appeared on Mari's face as she nodded.

'I see. A path that's no longer needed . . .'

From the basket, Jihoon took out an egg tart and bit into it. He stared at the fireflies as he spoke.

'. . . In a year, fireflies only glow for about two weeks. And after fourteen days, they'll disappear from the universe. It makes me think that we also don't get many chances in life to have a heart-to-heart . . . Will there even be fourteen nights where we can speak only the truth?'

The smile on Mari's face vanished. Jihoon had turned to face her, but she averted her gaze and sipped the champagne slowly. Seeing the stiffness in her jaw, Jihoon put down the egg tart and sat up straight.

'When I saw you there, sitting on the bench outside the

student cafeteria . . . I thought it was a lookalike, but my body reacted first. I felt a tingle at the back of my head, and it stopped me in my tracks. When I turned, you were staring at me. Ten whole years. You disappeared for all that time, and one day, you just popped up in front of me – as my colleague at the psychology research lab, no less. How should I put it? It's so *you*.'

Jihoon thought back to that day. The day when time started ticking again. He wanted to sit down for a heart-to-heart talk with Mari, but she'd find an excuse to slip away as soon as she sensed that he wanted to say more. When they bumped into each other at the lab, they would exchange pleasant greetings, sometimes talking about the weather of the day or the project, but Jihoon could tell that Mari was being guarded, as though there was an invisible chasm between them.

Now, he said nothing and simply stared at her. As if by doing so, he could dig up the traces of the passage of time. But he found himself unable to ask her anything. Nor could he tell what she was thinking. The walls in her eyes had risen higher.

Mari was the one who broke the silence. Acting like she had not disappeared for the last ten years, she told him that she was doing her master's in social psychology in the States and had come to Korea as an exchange student for a year. Jihoon heard the unspoken – she'd soon disappear again. Like a person who had never existed. A midsummer night's dream.

The fireflies flashed their lights in the dark. Jihoon sighed.

'Actually, I already knew that the book club would be discussing *Where the Crawdads Sing*. I've always hoped that you would read this book. When I read it, the first person I thought of was you.'

Mari swallowed hard. She wanted to say something in response, but words failed her. It was because she could feel the determination radiating from him. He was usually softly spoken and warm like toast, but once he set his heart on something, he was more determined than anyone else.

'That was before I saw you again. I imagined that you were somewhere in the world, perhaps under a different patch of sky, and how nice it'd be if the book could find its way to you.'

In their glasses, the nicely chilled champagne was sparkling a beautiful gold. Bubbles were rising one or two at a time. Jihoon sipped from his flute glass and let his gaze wander beyond the wetland to the mountain ridges. Above, the sky glowed a dark purple.

'. . . I thought you'd be comfortable in the marshlands of the story. What I'm saying is . . . I . . .' Jihoon struggled to finish his sentence.

Mari tucked her knees close to her and spoke. 'I . . . feel like I've been with you in the stories.'

Jihoon turned to look at her.

Why is my voice trembling? Mari wondered. She'd never been more nervous in her life. She tried to steady her pounding heart as she spoke. '*To Kill a Mockingbird, Anne of Green Gables, The Little Prince.* Do you remember those books? We read them in class.'

Mari thought back to her favourite quotes, the feeling of flipping through the pages of the well-thumbed copies from the library. Jihoon nodded.

'Of course. Remember the time I spilt some orange juice on *The Little Prince*?'

'Oh yeah. Was it the page about the baobabs on his planet?'

'I think it's the bit where he's speaking to the rose. And remember how we had to write a review of *Anne of Green Gables?* We thought we were smart by deciding to read only half the book and tell each other what went on in the other half.'

'That's because Anne really talks a lot. That book's thick.'

'Yeah, she speaks in paragraphs.'

Mari looked at the smiling Jihoon, and in her heart, she continued. *I wanted to tell you everything, too. I had so much to tell you . . .*

She poured herself another glass of champagne.

'And *To Kill a Mockingbird* reminds me of Christmas dinners at your place. Was it because we had to complete that assignment right before the Christmas break?'

Jihoon nodded. 'I remember that,' he murmured.

Travelling down memory lane made her heart ache.

'Jihoon, I . . . You know? Somehow it feels like you've been by my side these past ten years. Even if we weren't actually seeing each other . . . revisiting the books we read together made me feel your presence. I remember everything – the weather, how I felt, even what we were drinking as we read.'

Mari looked down at the sneakers on her feet.

'. . . I just want to say, you've always been my friend – even in the past ten years. Even if we were apart.'

Jihoon mulled over her words, that they'd always been friends . . . He gazed up at her with a confused look. 'But we could've been friends who met up with each other. Or . . . did I do something to make you upset?'

'Of course not! No way, I'm sure you know it too,' Mari said hurriedly. She sighed.

'Just that . . . I know it's impossible to pretend in front of you. I cannot act like everything's fine, I can't talk about the lovely parents I pretend I have. You will be able to see through me if I start acting like an innocent girl who dreams of getting married and starting my own family. With you, I can never live in my lies and keep up the image I want to portray . . .'

'Mari, all of us tell lies from time to time. Sometimes it's to protect ourselves, to protect others, or simply to escape from reality.'

Mari slowly looked up at him. She realised she was trembling. Her lips were quivering, and it was as if someone had splashed milk all over her thoughts, turning everything into an opaque white.

'Jihoon . . .'

Mari thought she ought to say something, but no sound came out. The fireflies flashed their green light, blinking.

Jihoon fixed his gaze on her.

'To be honest, I've heard a little about you every now and then. But you have never once opened up to me. I wondered if it's because you weren't ready to talk to me. I decided to ignore all the rumours and wait until you were ready. I had hoped that someday, you'd be able to tell me in your own time, in your own way. But it seems like you had no intention of doing that at all.'

Jihoon thought back to the summer night in Leipzig when he felt utterly defeated.

***

'By the way, I saw Mari. I bumped into her in the cafeteria at Boston Uni. About like three months ago?'

Jihoon felt his heart freeze. It was the fifth summer after Mari had vanished from his life. That evening, he was having dinner with his ex-classmates from the international school. Over beers, they were sharing updates on their life, and Jason, who had recently gone on an exchange programme to the States, brought up Mari.

'Really? How is she?' someone asked.

'Married, I think. Not that she told me, but woah, that

wedding ring. I swear I've never seen a bigger diamond in real life. She said she had to rush off somewhere, so we basically said hi and bye.'

Jason was still going on about Mari, but Jihoon wasn't listening.

Married . . .

It was as though he was walking on the street when someone suddenly punched him in the face. He'd never thought that Mari would be married. He got up abruptly, and headed out to the terrace of the pub, leaving behind the noise.

The midsummer nights of Leipzig were warm, but right now, Jihoon was numb to the heat and the noise. Mari's face flashed across his mind – the little girl he'd met at the museum, the classmate who stared at him on his first day at the new school, her joining his family's Christmas dinners.

After that fateful night, Jihoon changed his plans. He no longer wanted to stay in Germany and pursue his master's degree. Instead, he returned to Korea and enlisted. After his discharge from the military, he continued to stay in the country. There was no way he was going to run into Mari here. He just wanted, no, *needed*, a new environment. A place where he'd not be able to find a single trace of Mari . . .

***

Mari sat with her knees pulled close to her chest.

Jihoon spoke. 'I wanted to be honest with you today. Come to think of it, there are also things that I haven't told you. I don't know if I'll even have two weeks with you, so I just want to tell you how I feel.'

He tried to keep his tone even, but Mari knew that he was shaking.

'Mari, I care a lot for you. I want to protect you, and your many secrets. I want to tell you this, before it's too late and you disappear on me once more.'

His feelings were like a crate that had sunk into the sea a long time ago and finally resurfaced, bobbing up and down in choppy waters.

From his backpack, Jihoon took out a small box. It was the size of a ring box. Mari froze. She watched Jihoon open the box, and inside was a yellow butterfly mounted in a glass case.

'Berlin Museum of Natural History. The lobby. Remember that day? I met you for the first time when I was eight. You were staring so intensely at me and my parents that I couldn't help but turn back. And even when we went into the butterfly room, all I could remember was your eyes. Your empty and lonely eyes, and somehow that reminds me of the butterfly specimens on display. From then on, whenever I see taxidermised animals, I can't help but think of you, and how you seemed to be trapped in a tall, strong fortress. I don't know what's trapping you, or what's causing you so much pain, but isn't it time to let go?'

'Jihoon . . . I . . .'

The tears brimming in her eyes flowed down her cheeks. Mari stared at the butterfly in the case. Suddenly, she buried her face into her hands and started sobbing. This was the first time she had cried aloud in front of someone else.

Jihoon leaned in slowly and hugged her, a gentle hug like he was holding on to a friend who was having a hard time. Mari was like a tiny bird struggling to find its direction, its wings wet from flying through the clouds at dawn. Jihoon patted her gently, and in his gentle rhythm, Mari could feel what he wanted to tell her.

Mari, it's okay. It's okay . . .

It was quite a while later when they finally walked back up to the path where the bugs and cicadas were chirping. In the warm, humid air, they could smell the freshness of grass. Fireflies weaved in and out quietly. And in the dark forest, perhaps there were butterflies dancing too. It felt as though they had fallen into a dream, or a moment of déjà vu. Jihoon and Mari walked side by side in silence, and suddenly, they stopped at the same time. At the end of the path was a bright light.

Mari's lashes, wet with tears, were fluttering as she spoke.

'Jihoon . . . I must apologise. I'm sorry it's taken me ten years to say I'm sorry. You know . . . I'm very guarded. I get a kick out of people falling for my façade. I've been living for so long in my made-up world that I've lost sight of my real self . . . I created a persona, wanting to appear like I'm doing well, and that's how I've been living – a life of lies and half-truths.'

Jihoon opened his mouth as if to say something, but in the end, he fell silent. After a moment's pause, Mari continued.

'But in front of you, it's impossible to lie. And I don't want to. Even the thought of lying makes me hate myself. In the past decade, there were many times I could've just reached out, but in the end, I didn't. I was scared that if you knew the truth, even you'd abandon me. Or perhaps I just don't want to drag you into my problems. My life's a huge mess . . . I know it sounds like an excuse . . .'

Mari tried to hold back her tears.

'Ripley Syndrome . . . You've heard of that, right?' Mari asked, but she didn't wait for an answer. The words came out in a rush. 'Yes . . . that's me. I live in my own imaginary world, a complex world of lies. In fact, I don't even feel like I'm telling lies. I'm just portraying the image I want to have, what's so wrong with that? I believed that was the real me. But two years ago, there was a huge mess and . . . I was diagnosed with Ripley Syndrome. Of course, I refused to accept it at first. I've spent my life believing that the world I'd created was real. To acknowledge the diagnosis was to unravel everything I have, and it took a long time. I'm still seeing the . . . psychiatrist . . . getting treated . . .'

Jihoon nodded slowly, as if trying to tell her that everything was okay. He didn't ask any more questions. Instead, he held tightly onto her trembling hand. Jihoon had chosen to major in psychology because he wanted to understand what she was thinking. Now that he thought about it, perhaps she'd done the same because she was curious about her own feelings, too.

Hand in hand, they walked to the end of the path, where the lights of Soyangri Book Kitchen shone brightly.

***

'How was everything?' Siwoo asked as he walked into the book café carrying bags of rubbish from the wedding reception. Serin was seated at one of the tables, looking out at Jihoon and Mari, who were walking back and chatting at the same time.

Without taking her eyes off them, Serin replied, 'Not sure yet. They're coming back now.'

Serin wished she could see their expressions, but they were still a distance away. From the way they were walking, it didn't seem like they were particularly excited, nor were they awkwardly stiff.

'That guy . . . Jihoon, right? He's quite amazing, huh?'
'Indeed . . .'

Suddenly, Serin wondered if Namwoo had a side to him that she had never seen when they were together.

'Heading up north to Gangwon Province, and then all the

way down south to Muju County . . . just to find the fireflies. That's truly some major effort,' she said.

'Oh yeah, but does she know?' Siwoo asked, tying up the rubbish bags as he watched the two of them. 'That he went all over the country for more than a month in search of fireflies, just for her?'

'He's not the type who'll boast about his efforts. Same with the book club. He was the one who really wanted her to read the book and pleaded with us not to push it back to another day because he really wanted to tell her something tonight.'

'. . . I wonder if she'll ever realise how much he loves her.'

Nobody knew if the story that they'd been a part of would wind up with a happy or a sad ending. Just as it was impossible to pinpoint the direction of a spinning top. It was hard to see where things might lead them.

As the night deepened, the temperature dropped. The moon shone brightly in the sky. Outside, the fireflies were dancing, as if to a melody.

5

THE SECOND FRIDAY OF OCTOBER, 6 A.M.

Life was always on Min Soohyuk's side. Or at least it had been until he turned twenty. Soohyuk grew up in a mansion in Yeonhui-dong where his doting maternal grandpa would personally chauffeur him every day in his black imported sedan to the prestigious private kindergarten he attended.

Growing up, he was easily a head taller than his peers. He was well built and had a good appetite. Wherever he went, he was naturally the leader. Had he been born in the Joseon dynasty, he would've been a warrior. Sometimes, he could be hot-headed, or a little self-righteous, but he was a people person at heart. In elementary school, he moved to the affluent East Ichon-dong neighbourhood along the Han River. But like all other kids, he loved his tteokbokki, with an additional order of deep-fried seaweed rolls stuffed with glass noodles that he'd dip into the spicy sauce before finishing up with a bowl of ramyeon.

Soohyuk thought he lived a normal life. Only when he grew older did he realise how privileged he had been. His classmates hailed from renowned families – the who's who of political and business circles. At their school, the parents weren't blindly trusting of private education. Instead of solely focusing on academic achievements, there was also an

III

emphasis on nurturing their talents and hobbies, so he was spared from the dreariness of being shuttled to and from cram schools.

Soohyuk grew up to be a bright and cheerful kid. Whenever he saw his friends looking depressed or dispirited, he'd be truly puzzled. Romance came easy to him. He had smooth, clear skin and was great at sports, so naturally he caught the attention of many girls. He went on to date a few, partly because he was curious about love. Life was like a glitzy shopping mall; if he stretched out his hand, he could have anything he wanted.

He did well enough to get into a university in Seoul, but he knew that his father wasn't satisfied.

His one fear in life was his father. His parents had married out of love, but back then, his mother's family owned one of the biggest conglomerates in Korea. While it wasn't like in the dramas, where his mother would be forced into a political marriage, her family insisted that her partner learn the ropes of the business. His father, a vocal performance major, had dreamed of becoming a tenor singer. But in the eighties, it was almost impossible to make a decent living as a performer. His father knew his in-laws had good intentions, so he gave up his dream and devoted himself to the corporate world.

His father turned out to be a natural at it. He was a sharp businessman who instinctively knew how to sniff out a good deal. Instead of attending breakfast meetings with other second-generation chaebol executives or going for closed-door seminars on Korea's economic development, he chose to keep a close eye on financial metrics. Numbers never lie. He pushed ahead with tough personnel decisions, and in his quest to steer the company to greater heights, he had no qualms cutting old friendships if they proved to be a burden.

That made Soohyuk fearful of his father. His father

scorned relationships built on love and camaraderie; he would never allow such emotions to cloud his judgement. For more than thirty years, he maintained a strong authority, and his management style had unconsciously seeped into his parenting style. To Soohyuk, his father was like an impenetrable wall of steel; raining punches on him wouldn't leave the slightest scratch. Unbeknownst to Soohyuk, his father was worried about him. Having grown up carefree and bright, would he be able to withstand the storms of life? Until he turned twenty, life was like a red carpet that unfurled for Soohyuk wherever he went. If one day he found himself in the wilderness, would he be able to survive?

Soohyuk's father had never demanded anything of him or scolded him. Yet the iron stronghold he wielded over his own life felt like a subtle message to him:

You're such a pushover. The world is a thunderstorm, how are you going to survive when you're soft like a peach? Come to your senses.

Growing up, Soohyuk's interactions with his father were always short, somewhat formal affairs. Even then, he found the pressure overwhelming. His father always seemed to be upset with him, and he grew up convinced that his father had marked him as someone who'd never be able to meet his expectations.

His mother, on the other hand, was like the calm ocean in his life. Spending time with her was like taking a walk on the beach in the gentle sunlight. He could tell his mother everything. When he quit university in his freshman year and wanted to study abroad in New York to become a musical director, his mother was the one who helped him find a good school, an apartment and made sure he had a generous living allowance. She convinced his father to let him go, reminding him of his own dreams to become a tenor singer. Smiling, she pointed out that their son was also trying to fight for his dreams. When he returned from New York, his father wanted him to join the company. If not for his mother insisting otherwise, perhaps Soohyuk might have given in.

But the first cracks in his perfect life appeared when the realisation hit him – he just wasn't talented enough. None of his scripts made it to stage production. He failed at every screenwriting competition he submitted to. The jury didn't provide feedback, but he thought he knew why. He couldn't bring out the different flavours in life – the sadness, obstacles and pain. Without the emotional depth, naturally, his stories couldn't connect to the audience.

Just as he was getting anxious about his string of failures, a friend approached him with an opportunity to invest in a musical. The friend was looking to do a Korean production of a musical from overseas, and he suggested that Soohyuk could direct it. Thinking that he could finally show his father some achievements, he sold off part of the stocks inherited from his grandfather and pumped the money into the project. However, the very next day, the guy went radio silent.

That was how he was forced to join his father at the company. His younger sister, who had been there for more than five years, was going to be promoted to a team leader next year. The work was boring. Not that he had a lot to do or very challenging projects (everyone was eager to help him anyway). Time was trickling away like the sand in an hourglass, trapping him within. Sleep evaded him. Out of nowhere, his heart started racing and heat flushed to his face. The symptoms only got worse with time. But he refused to see a psychiatrist or therapist; he was too proud to do that. Instead, on the weekend, he'd drive out to the lake or sea and spend a few hours sitting alone and emptying his mind.

That was how he pulled through each day. But one day, the final blow came. His mother passed away. She'd battled with laryngeal cancer for a while, but luckily, it was discovered early, and she was later declared cancer-free. However, in a follow-up examination, she did a CT scan, and the doctors found out that she had lung cancer, well into stage three. She'd seemed like her usual self, but three months after the diagnosis, she passed away suddenly. Unlike his maternal grandmother, who had fought Alzheimer's for eight years, this time, he didn't manage to say a proper goodbye.

Soohyuk's world crumbled. He couldn't accept what had happened. Why did life lead him to a dead-end; why was peace and happiness pulled from him without warning? He had neither the energy nor the resolve to even think of where everything had gone wrong.

***

Soohyuk started to contemplate death. Quietly. It wasn't like he'd drunk-dial his friends at ungodly hours and scream, 'I want to die!' But like running water in a bathtub, the intrusive thoughts gradually filled his mind. He didn't see any point in carrying on. The weight of everything pressed down upon him, and once the scales tipped, much like the moment the bathtub overflowed, it'd be time to leave the world.

On the second Friday in October, Soohyuk didn't turn up to work. Nobody understood him; not that he understood himself either. He barely recognised the cold, hard face in the mirror. At six in the morning, Soohyuk got into his car and drove off. The humming engine and the spaciousness of his car always gave him comfort. Perhaps because it reminded him of the good old times sitting in his grandfather's black sedan.

The sun had yet to rise. The world, painted a bluish tinge, was still snoozing. Soohyuk didn't have a destination in mind. But since he'd gone to the beach last week, perhaps the mountains this time? And if he felt better mid-drive, he might head into the office.

Just then he thought of something he'd seen on his friend's Instagram, about an art gallery that was holding a New York-themed exhibition – the city he'd spent his twenties in. Soohyuk searched for the post and set his destination as Suhwajin Art Gallery, 147 kilometres away from Seoul.

Along the drive, the memories of the midsummer heat in New York came flooding back. Sylvia in hotpants eating a mint-chocolate cone, laughing and walking down the streets of Chelsea. Next to her, Hyungguk in a permanent scowl. The three of them in front of SoHo's art galleries, waxing lyrical about a scene from a movie. Soohyuk chuckled at the memory before catching himself. It was the first time in six months, ever since his mother's death, that he had genuinely smiled.

The art gallery didn't open until noon, but his car had already turned into the car park just after eight. He parked and got out. Behind the gallery was a bamboo forest and when the wind blew, the leaves rustled like the waves. Out of nowhere, two spotted wild cats emerged before nipping out of sight. Soohyuk felt a curious sensation, as though he'd arrived at the edge of time. The wind ruffled his hair, and the quiet surroundings, as if glad of the company, enveloped him in an embrace.

A sense of peace permeated the empty grounds. The cool air and the warm sunlight in the autumn morning left a curious sensation on his skin. He paused his footsteps. A mix of happiness and sadness welled over him. Had the world always been so beautiful? So dazzlingly bright? Yet, he also felt a lingering grief. The autumns he'd spent with his mother could now only exist as memories, things of the past.

He felt a tingle at the back of his head; tears threatened to spill. Here, miles away from the city, where not a single soul was in sight, perhaps it was okay to let himself go. Until the heavy sadness in him could melt away.

Soohyuk returned to the car, put on his shades and started the playlist he often listened to in New York. He thought he'd burst into tears, but the hum of the engine calmed his heart instead. He was craving a hot Americano.

***

After getting Hyungjun's help to finish up with the breakfast preparation, Siwoo took the food he'd set aside for the stray cats and took a walk to the art gallery. He hadn't expected to see anyone at this hour, but at the car park, a man got out of his car and was looking around.

The first thing that caught Siwoo's eyes was the man's watch. It stood out against his casual shirt and cotton pants. Even from a distance, he could make out two moving cogs and the encrusted jewels on the dial that glittered in the sunlight. With his smooth, tanned skin, it was hard to tell his age. He was tall, at least 180 cm, and from his broad shoulders, Siwoo guessed that the man hit the gym regularly.

Their gazes met and Siwoo could sense the man getting flustered. His eyes were hidden behind his dark shades, but there was something awkward about his movements that reminded Siwoo of a giant middle-school student who has accidentally walked into the wrong classroom at the start of the school year. What was this man in oversized shades and an expensive-looking watch doing out here in front of the bamboo forest? At such an early hour too.

The man took off his sunglasses and called out to Siwoo. 'Excuse me, is there a restaurant or snack shop nearby?'

'Nowhere that's open at this hour. They all start at about eleven,' Siwoo replied. Was this man an art collector? he wondered.

A tabby cat appeared, meowing at Siwoo. It must've smelt the food. A distance away, a grey cat was also solemnly looking his way.

'I see. Thank you.' The man was starting to walk away, but Siwoo called out to him.

'If you don't mind homecooked food, would you like to join us for breakfast at our guesthouse? I work there. It's just adding a spoon to the table, no trouble to us at all.'

Soohyuk looked at the man, who flashed him a friendly grin. Over the years, he'd grown used to trusting only himself, but this man who was feeding the stray cats didn't look like a murderer or scammer. And the mention of *homecooked food* touched something in his heart. He remembered going home to the delicious smell of freshly cooked rice, beef braised in soy sauce, egg rolls and a hearty soybean paste stew. His mother's side profile was etched in his mind like a photo. Suddenly, he felt a gnawing hunger.

***

The staff area was on the second floor, above the book café. The spread was even better than Soohyuk had imagined. The soybean stew with clams and mussels was fragrant and at the same time a little spicy, perhaps from the peppers. Crunchy fresh cabbage was paired with a ssamjang dipping sauce that was made from soybean paste available only in the countryside. The mackerel was grilled to a golden brown, and next to the egg rolls with colourful bits of carrots and broccoli were the banchan of cubed radish kimchi and yeolmu kimchi made from young radish leaves.

Neither the owner, Yoojin, nor Siwoo asked him anything. Not even for his name. Soohyuk greeted them shyly before sitting down. But somehow, he didn't feel the least bit uncomfortable joining them for breakfast.

Behind the two of them was a large window which framed the meandering mountain ridges and the beautiful autumn landscape. It was a fair-weather day, and whenever the wind blew, he watched the leaves swaying in slow motion. Sometimes, one or two would drop to the ground. The autumn colours outside were a perfect complement to the white wood furniture inside the guesthouse.

Soohyuk thought he must have eaten twice his usual portion. He refilled his rice and polished off the remaining side dishes and stew when they were done.

Yoojin excused herself as she had to double-check the list of books that were arriving today and prepare for an event in the afternoon. Siwoo made to follow Yoojin. As he got up, he flashed his signature smile at Soohyuk, inviting him to have a cup of coffee at the café before he headed off.

'I'll take care of the plates,' Soohyuk said.

'Oh no. Just leave it. We'll do it later with the rest.'

'But . . . I'll feel better if you let me help.'

'Alright . . . go ahead, thanks!'

Soohyuk took out his phone and put on 'Lost Stars' from the movie soundtrack of *Begin Again*, humming to the melody as he did the dishes. He didn't mind doing it; in fact, he enjoyed it. Plates stained with kimchi liquid, the rice bowls with bits of rice stuck to the rim, the soup bowls with dregs. As he ran them under hot water, scrubbed them clean and let them dry at room temperature, it was as though the stains on his heart were also being washed away. He felt refreshed, like returning from a long, leisurely walk. He loved how he could put aside his thoughts in front of the sink.

With everything stacked neatly on the drying rack, Soohyuk sat down on the fabric sofa and stared out the windows as he listened to the songs playing on the app. He let his mind go blank. The sky was a perfect blue, as though someone had cut and pasted colour paper above. An aeroplane flew past, leaving a white track which slowly faded away.

Through the opened windows, the wind rushed in. The occasional leaf rode the breeze as branches swayed in a dance. Soohyuk found himself walking down memory lane – he was on the way home from a practice session for the autumn sports meet and the wind was cooling his sweat-stained face. The humidity of summer had receded. The air was dry, with a touch of coolness, as if heralding the onset of autumn. It was yet another change in seasons. Indeed, even when life felt like teetering on the edge of the cliff, time continued to flow. Even when he was struggling in a swamp of emotions that he refused to show anyone else, even if his mother was no longer in this world, autumn continued to dazzle with its colours.

Heading downstairs to the book café, the first thing he noticed was the high ceilings and the rich aroma of coffee mixed with the scent of books. Siwoo was unpacking boxes; the other staff were also busy, checking the inventory of books and merchandise like the recyclable totes and notepads. Next to the shelves there was a stretch of windows slightly below eye level, framing the beautiful scenery outside.

'Thank you for breakfast. I can't remember the last time I had such a hearty meal,' said Soohyuk

Yoojin flashed him a gentle smile. She could sense that his heart was a lot lighter than when he first arrived this morning.

'Our staff member is as good as a professional chef. It's impossible to think of dieting with him around. So glad that the countryside breakfast is to your liking. I'll get you a cup of coffee. Feel free to browse the books in the meantime,' Yoojin said breezily.

Soohyuk's face reddened slightly. 'Thank you.'

The shelves weren't crammed full of books. Instead, it felt like someone had taken the time and effort to curate a collection and organise them according to themes. His eyes landed on the couple of novels right in the centre – 'October Healing Reads'. To the left was a selection of essay and poetry collections and on the right, colourful fairy-tale books. In front of the bookshelves was a small green chalkboard sign quoting a line from *Anne of Green Gables*.

'I'm so glad I live in a world where there are Octobers. It would be terrible if we just skipped from September to November, wouldn't it. Look at these maple branches. Don't they give you a thrill – several thrills? I'm going to decorate my room with them.'

His sister would've loved this. She was such a huge fan of the book. Two years younger than him, she was always a ray of sunshine, someone who never shied away from expressing her feelings. He thought affectionately of how she had displayed her *Anne of Green Gables* DVD boxset in her room, as though it was her most prized possession, dusting it every day for fear of getting a single speck of dirt on it. The cartoon used to air on TV in the morning and because she'd insist on catching the whole episode, she was almost always late for elementary school. The number of times she'd argued with Mum! Soohyuk thought fondly.

He could still hum the melody of the opening soundtrack. Thinking of the song unlocked another memory – his sister sat rooted in front of the TV. Mum was next to her on the sofa, cupping a mug of coffee and occasionally taking a sip while keeping her eyes on the screen. Occasionally, their eyes would widen, and they'd chuckle in unison.

The other day, he'd bumped into his sister at the office. At first look, she seemed to be her usual self, but he could tell that she'd lost weight, and the light in her eyes had been extinguished. It'd be nice to have a chat with her over a glass of wine, but ever since their mother died, he hadn't spoken to her one on one at all.

Soohyuk stared at the book cover. For the first time, he wondered if his sister was also feeling as lonely and sad as he was. If Anne were here, what would she say to his sister?

He picked up the hardcover novel and flipped through the pages, pausing at something that Anne said.

'. . . When I left Queen's my future seemed to stretch out before me like a straight road. I thought I could see along it for many a milestone. Now there is a bend in it. I don't know what lies around the bend, but I'm going to believe that the best does. It has a fascination of its own, that bend, Marilla. I wonder how the road beyond it goes – what there is of green glory and soft, checkered light and shadows – what new landscapes – what new beauties – what curves and hills and valleys further on.'

Soohyuk held on to the book as he continued browsing. It had been a long time since he'd stepped into a bookshop. Next to *Anne of Green Gables*, the staff had recommended a few more book-pairings for the novel, alongside a handwritten note.

[Take a leisurely walk in the woods of words]
#goodmoodreads #healingessays #koreanauthors
#cosyreads

Reflections on Kindness by Kim Honbi
The Skill of Relaxation by Kim Hana
Hohoho by Yoon Ga-eun
The Taste of Kkwabaegi by Choi Minseok
The Charm of Kkawabaegi by Choi Minseok
It Doesn't Matter, Does It? by Jang Kiha

Noticing that a free wrapping service was available for customers who purchased three books or more, Soohyuk browsed over a couple of books before settling on Yoon Ga-eun's *Hohoho*. The cover illustration of a woman lying on the sofa reading comic books reminded him of his sister. He liked the subtitle too: *Stories about the things that made me laugh*. Next, he picked up Choi Minseok's *The Taste of Kkwabaegi*. The table of contents was enough to make him chuckle. He approached the counter with the three books, including *Anne of Green Gables*.

'You have a lovely bookshop,' he told Yoojin. 'I'll take these.'
'Sure. Are they a gift?'
'I'm thinking of giving them to my younger sister. She loved *Anne of Green Gables*.'
'Yeah, it's impossible not to fall in love with Anne,' Yoojin said as she expertly wrapped the books.
'By the way, how much should I pay for breakfast—'

'No worries at all.' Yoojin smiled as she gently cut him off. 'That's the breakfast service for the guests and the staff eat the same too. Just adding a spoon to the table doesn't cost us anything. And you even did the dishes for us! We should be the one thanking you.'

As if just remembering, Yoojin passed him a takeout cup. The rich aroma of Americano enveloped them.

'Enjoy the coffee as you wait for your books. I meant to pass you this just now, but look at me – I got distracted. I've been like this recently.'

Soohyuk smiled and took the cup with both hands.

'I was craving a coffee, so this is a godsend. Thank you.'

With the last book wrapped, Yoojin took a postcard and held it out along with the books to Soohyuk.

'Doesn't it feel like something's missing if you simply hand her the books? How about writing a note?'

On the postcard was an illustration of a man with a T-shirt that read: *Would you like to go on a picnic with me?* Soohyuk burst out laughing.

'Um. If I ask her to go on a picnic with me, she'd think an alien has possessed her brother.'

Yoojin chuckled but pushed the postcard to him all the same.

'I heard you came all the way from Seoul to visit the art gallery. Are you heading there soon? If so, can you do me a favour?'

Soohyuk spread out his hands, indicating that he was at her service. From his wide smile, Yoojin could tell that he grew up with lots of love. His harried expression from this morning had cleared. Yoojin picked up a box that contained a couple of books.

'Can you pass these to the curator of the Suhwajin Art

Gallery – Kim Woojin? And these brochures, too. They arrived this morning. I was thinking of making a trip later, but since you're heading there . . .'

'Of course, no problem at all.' Soohyuk smiled as he took the box.

To Kim Woojin-nim. The neat handwriting on the box reminded him of the vibes at Soyangri Book Kitchen. He paused for a moment before speaking.

'Um. By the way . . . I saw on your Instagram that there's going to be a persimmon- and chestnut-picking activity in the afternoon. Would you need an extra pair of hands? Let me help – take it as me paying for breakfast.'

Yoojin paused, a little surprised. With a mischievous glint in her eye, she looked him up and down, and chuckled.

'But do you know how to do it? And your clothes – you might have to throw them away after that . . .'

Only then did Soohyuk gaze down at his outfit. He was in his usual workwear – a shirt and beige cotton trousers. Casual, yet there wasn't a single speck of dust or even a stain on his well-pressed trousers. Definitely not the best clothes to wear for chestnut picking in the mountains. They burst out laughing.

***

The art gallery was smaller than expected, but strikingly futuristic. Soohyuk marvelled at the unique architecture that accentuated odd angles and lines instead of the usual square rooms. The maze-like structure added to the charm of exploring the gallery.

New York, viewed through the lens of the exhibition's curator, was a city that was carefree, yet painfully lonely. The beggars on the streets, too, had big dreams, but reality was harsh. As much as it was a welcoming place, most people would leave for elsewhere after struggling to make ends meet, while those who remained tried their best to hang on. The curator had weaved together a powerful narrative through different types of artworks, including black-and-white photos of NYC streets in the 1950s, stiff-looking hexagonal chairs, a painting of the view from the third-floor rooftop of the Metropolitan Museum of Art, a photo of a girl in an I ♡ NY T-shirt, as well as works of art on loan from MoMA.

Soohyuk found Kim Woojin. In an oversized T-shirt and washed-out jeans, he greeted Soohyuk with a bright smile. Soohyuk's first thought was that the man fit perfectly with this unique art gallery.

'Siwoo called. I heard you were here really early in the morning!'

'Oh . . . well. Anyway, here you go,' said Soohyuk as he passed him the box.

Woojin took out a brochure and examined it carefully, as if to check the feel of the design in print and to double-check if there were any typos.

'Thanks for saving me a trip! I was going to get it myself.'

Woojin's polished demeanour reminded him of a hotelier. Soohyuk nodded politely in response.

It was one in the afternoon. On a usual Friday, he'd be at the office at this time, but right now, he was in an art gallery in the mountains. It was as though he'd stepped into a different realm, where nothing – not the season, the date, the day of the week – mattered anymore. It occurred to him that, if he wanted, he could always take a day off on a weekday to visit the mountains or the beaches. But for the past year, not once did the thought of taking any time off cross his mind. Every day seemed to blend into the next, in a never-ending cycle. He was so exhausted that he simply couldn't think about anything else.

Just as he was about to leave, he paused and turned back to Woojin, who was looking at the books in the box.

'Excuse me, is there a place nearby that sells desserts?'

***

Thirty individually packed boxes of waffles filled Soyangri Book Kitchen with a sweet, delicious smell. Each of the thick waffles was drizzled in maple syrup, topped with fresh cream and dusted with cinnamon powder. A young boy who stepped in with his mother made a beeline for them, exclaiming in delight. Yoojin chuckled at the sight of the tower of waffles.

'Wow! Why did you get so many?'

'Payment for today's breakfast.'

Soohyuk grinned, but in fact, he was surprised at himself. For the past few months, he'd been a walking zombie, expressionless, speaking only when he absolutely had to. But right now, it felt like colours were returning to his life. Was it because he was reminded of his free-spirited twenties in NYC?

He'd have to return to reality soon, but in this moment, he was on a trip.

'I thought they'd make a nice treat for those participating in today's activity. For me, too. I need to replenish my sugar levels to have enough energy to help with the chestnut- and persimmon-picking.'

'I love the waffles from this shop! Did you get the vanilla ones too?'

Just as Yoojin was opening one of the boxes, Siwoo appeared by her side.

'These smell divine!'

He quickly scooped up three boxes and kept them behind the counter for the staff. Then, he held out a creased black T-shirt and a pair of patterned baggy trousers.

'Hyung-nim, time to change into work clothes.'

Soohyuk laughed as he took them, feeling like a musical actor about to go up on stage. He looked at the baggy trousers . . . but perhaps his colleagues might be more shocked to see him in a wrinkled T-shirt. And it had been so long since someone addressed him as *hyung-nim*. He liked being called an older brother. It made him feel close to Siwoo. Like a light autumn breeze, something soft brushed gently across his heart.

Facilitating the chestnut-picking activity was no mean feat. First, he had to shake the trees to make the burrs fall. Next he stamped his foot on the sharp-edged burrs to crack them open and pick out the perfect chestnuts, untouched by bugs. Several times, he got pricked. At the same time, he had to keep an eye on the running kids to make sure that they didn't fall and the sharp thorns didn't pierce through their clothing. Since the terrain was quite steep and there was also the danger of snakes, he had to be on alert all the time.

Unlike what others might have imagined, there was nothing remotely romantic or whimsical about it. It was hard work. Soohyuk was on his feet from two in the afternoon until sunset. After making sure that none of the participants were left behind, he was the last one to leave the mountain. It suddenly occurred to him that in the past four hours, he'd not touched his phone at all. Well, it didn't buzz, but neither did he think to reach for it.

The mountain, drenched in the colours of sunset, was a sight to behold. The cloudless sky was bidding the day goodbye; the branches of the plum blossom trees swayed in greeting. The persimmons they had picked today were hanging from the roof of the book kitchen.

Siwoo was sitting at one of the tables in the book café. Perhaps because he'd been hanging around with the kids here on a family staycation, he was deep in concentration watching a YouTube video and learning how to fold a car-shaped origami. By the shelves, customers were browsing the books like they were at an art exhibition. Looking into the café from the garden was like getting a glimpse into a peaceful magical village, Soohyuk thought.

'The trousers look good on you. You could pass as a local,' Yoojin said as she appeared next to him. He turned and smiled at her. Yoojin grinned back. Quietly, they stood shoulder to shoulder, gazing into the café.

After a while, she broke the silence. 'Thanks for helping us out. We were quite understaffed to be honest; we were just going to wing it somehow.'

She thought he might say something in response, but he remained quiet.

'I packed some sweet persimmons and chestnuts for you. Please take them back to Seoul and enjoy—'

'I'm hoping to stay for the weekend. Is there a room available?'

Once again, he surprised himself. He was a stickler for routine; he'd never go on an impromptu trip, certainly not without his shaving cream, cleanser . . . It wasn't just about toiletries, he didn't even have a change of underwear. What was he thinking? Logic yelled at him, but the words that tumbled from his mouth surprised him yet again.

'If all the rooms are full, I can sleep on a couch.'

He bit on his lip. His gaze was still fixed on the evening

landscape and the sunset that was painting the mountain a beautiful red.

'Oh . . .'

Yoojin glanced at him from the side. She sensed that he wasn't just speaking on a whim; there was desperation in his eyes. He seemed to be going through a precarious time, like a bird flapping its wings for the entire night in search of a resting spot, thoroughly exhausted.

Yoojin understood the need to retreat at times, to hide in a cave, away from sight, and from reality. She tried to keep her tone light.

'The rooms are full. I'm guessing you've seen our comfortable sofa in the staff living room? If that's okay with you, go ahead . . . but the second floor doesn't have curtains. The sun will be your alarm clock.'

Soohyuk smiled and let out a long breath of relief. He looked up. There were some grey clouds in the sky, but because the air was clear and fresh, it didn't feel dreary at all. The sun went down, blurring the edges of the mountain ridges and slowly, the sky dimmed as crisp autumn air moistened the ground.

'Hyung-nim! How could you sleep on the sofa? Come to my room!' Siwoo would not take no for an answer, and Soohyuk became his roommate for the weekend.

At dinnertime, the three of them sat around the table as Yoojin and Siwoo started to share, over much laughter, their childhood memories. Like how little Siwoo in nappies had sung and danced in the rain, how Yoojin in Grade 5 had written an embarrassing heartbreak poem after getting rejected by her crush; the memories of holidaying at Haeundae Beach in Busan in midsummer and feeding her friends saltwater; the day where the national university entrance exam results were released and how it had felt like the end of the world. Back then, they were all trying their best to figure out their path in life, and now these had turned into fond memories. Soohyuk didn't offer his own stories, but they didn't mind. They'd suspected that he might not be comfortable to share. Either way, they were happy with his company.

They ate until their stomachs were about to burst, and then headed out to the second-floor terrace. On the outdoor parasol table, they set up a portable induction stove to boil the chestnuts they'd washed downstairs. Soohyuk was impressed. As they waited for the chestnuts to cook slowly, they poured the wine. Siwoo, a beer aficionado, was already on his second can.

A crescent moon hung in the clear sky. The dazzling sun had left the stage, replaced by a night of lingering feelings. The wind was quiet like a prowling cat.

'... Have you ever had such thoughts while driving?' Soohyuk spoke softly. Yoojin, who was rolling a couple of warm chestnuts in her palm, looked up. Next to her, Siwoo was already dozing off.

'Imagine yourself speeding down the seaside road with a view of the emerald sea. The weather is fair, not a single wisp of clouds in the sky. A perfect day to play a song like Coldplay's "Viva la Vida". You feel the beat – in the music, in your heart – and nothing else seems to matter. You cruise down the road, bobbing your head to the rhythm. In the distance, a white wild goose flies across the sky. You make a turn, only to be confronted by a big container truck driving at full speed towards you. And *bam!* The scene goes black.'

The pot on the induction cooker gurgled. Soohyuk didn't wait for Yoojin's answer. She, too, sensed that he had more to say.

'One night, I went to visit my friend at the hospital. He was driving along the expressway at dawn when he suddenly had a panic attack and rammed into the guardrail. No life-threatening injuries, but he broke his arm and rib . . . He refused to see any visitors. I don't know why, but when I think of him, I think about this scene.'

Yoojin knew that he was, in fact, referring to himself. It wasn't just her suspicion. The look in his eyes told her everything – the dream-like sequence was reflected in his pupils.

Yoojin downed the last mouthful of the sparkling wine. In the distance, the night-calls of the autumn bugs pulsed like a heartbeat.

'It's the perfect time to dive into a Douglas Kennedy novel.'

The night had quietened. The insects, perhaps tired out from the incessant calls, hummed softly. Soohyuk slowly turned at Yoojin's words.

'Douglas Kennedy? Who's that?'

'An author, of course.'

Soohyuk chuckled. His laughter sounded like ripples appearing on a calm lake. Siwoo was fast asleep on the sofa. Just a moment ago, he was bragging about how downing five cans of beers was no big deal for him. Yoojin pulled up a blanket around his shoulders before sitting down again.

'What you just described reminds me of his novels. It starts with a protagonist who leads a successful life but feels empty on the inside. Then, something small triggers them to throw away everything and leave behind their old life to settle in a village in the countryside. They change their name, appearance, career, and live as a completely different person.'

Yoojin paused to adjust her breathing, and she glanced at him to see if he was listening. Even though he was completely still, she could tell that she had his attention.

'I like the idea of hiding myself in a place where nobody knows me, and starting a brand-new life,' she said, smiling.

Soohyuk didn't reply.

'Whenever I find myself getting upset or angry, I reach for a book that allows me to immerse fully in another world – maybe like a crime or fantasy novel. They're my painkillers. In those moments I'm absorbed in a book, I can forget the pain of reality. It's as if the characters are saying: *Life can get so ridiculous at times, right? You didn't expect it to be so bad, huh?*'

Yoojin saw the loneliness in Soohyuk's eyes, like a lotus flower blooming quietly at dawn before fading away. Finally, he spoke.

'That's the first time I've heard someone describing books as painkillers.'

He broke into a smile, and in that moment, Yoojin saw the young, playful boy in him, unlike the colourless impression he'd given her so far. It was as if a bright and warm personality tucked deep inside him was resurfacing.

'. . . Um. Well, there's a song I always listen to when I'm upset or angry,' Soohyuk said softly. A gentle light lit up his eyes. 'It's "Waltz for Debby". My mum loved that jazz song. When she baked apple pies, she'd put on Bill Evans's rendition on the vinyl record player, listening to it on repeat from the time she made the pastry till she popped the pie into the oven.'

As he recalled the melody, it was as if he could smell her bakes in the air, hear her humming the tune in front of the oven. Soohyuk wanted to say more, but it was hard to put his thoughts into words, so he paused. Yoojin was awash with a sense of relief. If he'd been wandering aimlessly in the dark, in this moment, it felt as though he was learning to look up at the night sky.

'Oh? I should listen to it,' she said lightly.

Yoojin searched for the song on the app and played it. The waltz music blended in with the calls of the birds in the distance. Shrouded behind the rainclouds, the moon peeked out occasionally, before disappearing again.

***

Soohyuk opened his eyes and was greeted by the bright sunshine. For a moment, he was confused as to whether he was in a dream or reality. The space was unfamiliar, and the surroundings were strangely quiet, almost like being in a soundproofed room. Out of habit, he reached for his phone and checked the time. 11.12 a.m. He hadn't slept in for a long time.

Soohyuk looked around Siwoo's room. The sun was streaming in through the windows. The first thing he noticed was the poster of the singer Diane on the wall, and the Polaroid photos pegged to a string across the wall, mostly landscape pictures of Soyangri Book Kitchen. There was an assortment of objects strewn on the floor – sweatshirts, socks and two big cardboard boxes. The owner was nowhere to be seen. Oh right. Siwoo had mentioned that he'd usually wake up at six to prepare the guests' breakfast. Soohyuk remained lying in bed. He blinked.

I could get used to this life.

For the first time in a while, his mind was clear.

The first writers' studio session had just ended by the time he stepped into the book café with stubble on his face. Yoojin was at the writers' space typing away at her laptop. Noticing him, she waved in greeting and gestured that he would find Siwoo at the counter.

Siwoo, who'd just finished reshelving the books, greeted him warmly. 'Hyung-nim! Did you have a good night's rest? I kept some food for you from the breakfast buffet. I'll bring it to you at the backyard table.'

Soohyuk couldn't believe that he'd only known Yoojin and Siwoo for less than forty-eight hours. They felt more familiar than the colleagues with whom he'd worked for the past year. He watched Siwoo approach the backyard holding a tray filled with an assortment of items – an apple, a croissant, yoghurt topped with strawberries and nuts. The autumn sun was strong, but the overhead branches of the plum blossom trees provided enough shade. The wind blew, carrying the aroma of coffee from the takeout stand. Soohyuk absentmindedly turned his gaze towards the mountain where they'd gone chestnut-picking yesterday. Yoojin appeared with a drip coffee pot in hand.

'Chestnut ajusshi, you must've been totally knocked out this morning. I thought you'd be up by ten.'

Even teasing each other felt natural.

'My strategy is to combine breakfast and lunch so I don't have to pay so much for my meals,' he joked.

Laughing, Yoojin poured some coffee into his mug. The rich aroma blended well with the smell of grass and plants. The rainclouds from last night were completely gone. The sky was a brilliant blue. Soohyuk sipped his coffee.

'Is there a scenic drive route around here?'

Yoojin paused for a moment.

'There's a metasequoia-lined road further down – about one kilometre away, turn right at the intersection and you'll see it. It's the trendy spot now. In the past, the residents used to drive along the winding road to the highway, but seven years ago, when a new straight road was built in the next neighbourhood, people stopped using that winding road. Not long ago, it was featured as a filming location for a car TV ad and the ending scene of a drama. So now it's popular again. It's a very picturesque drive, even if the bends in the road are a little dizzying.'

And under her breath, she added: *Not the coastal road that you can speed down at 200 km per hour.*

From the side, Yoojin watched him as he searched for the place on his phone.

There won't be any oncoming truck. If you aren't on the lookout for that, it's quite a nice drive.

He looked up, as if he'd heard her, and gave her a relaxed smile.

It wasn't quite like speeding on the expressway, but he enjoyed a relaxed drive along the highway. The bends in the road felt like a ride on a kids' Viking ship. As he drove up the slope, he admired the metasequoia trees on both sides, watching as the autumn leaves fell. As he cruised downhill, it was as if he had left his anxiety behind.

An old memory surfaced. He was visiting his grandfather at his Yeonhui-dong mansion, and after lunch, he was going to the nearby supermarket with his mum. It was a downhill walk, passing through winding alleyways. Soohyuk remembered that it was autumn back then too. He squinted in the sunlight, and the cloudless sky was a plain blue. He ran downhill and felt himself gain speed as if the wind was pushing him from behind. *Woohoo!* little Soohyuk yelled.

His mum ran after him, telling him to be careful. She must've also felt the force pushing her forward. The wind blew, carrying her scent.

Soohyuk stopped the car by the road, and stared into the distance, as if he could still see the receding figures of a mother and child running down the hill.

Two hours later, Soohyuk returned to Soyangri Book Kitchen, his face visibly relaxed. Watching Yoojin and Siwoo come out to greet him, he realised in that moment that he had made new friends.

Soohyuk was used to keeping his walls high. He found it hard to trust, and it had only got worse in the last five years, as if he was always in a battlefield, careful not to fall for anyone's tricks. Behind every friendly smile was a more calculating intent. He'd been conditioned to think that way.

However, in Soyangri Book Kitchen, it somehow felt okay to be letting down his guard. The group here generously invited him to share a warm homecooked meal. They didn't demand any explanations from him; there was much chatter and laughter. He even found himself sharing his mother's favourite jazz song.

Soohyuk sat in a corner of the book café and opened the book that Yoojin had just gifted him. *Murakami Radio* – an essay collection from Haruki Murakami. On a sticky note on the opening page of 'Shaving at Night', she wrote: *I swear I'm not hinting at you to shave! Heh.*

For a moment, he was confused. Then he raised a hand to his chin and felt the prickly stubble. Chuckling, he turned the page and started reading slowly. Outside, the Saturday evening sun was setting.

***

The next day, a Sunday, Yoojin, Soohyuk and Siwoo spent the first light sitting at the long bench by the lake, watching the sun rise as the fog dissipated completely. Everyone was silent. In his own way, Soohyuk was bidding goodbye to the book kitchen, to Yoojin and Siwoo. He didn't have to say anything, but the two of them understood. Sitting shoulder to shoulder, they stared out at the lake, nodding occasionally. Soohyuk was leaving that morning. An appropriate goodbye at an appropriate distance.

It was time to return to daily life. The time spent at the book kitchen was filled with warmth and comfort, like enjoying the first sunshine in a long while, or a gentle and steady breath. Yet it wasn't like his life was completely changed. For now, the time of wearing wrinkled T-shirts and not shaving must come to an end.

On the expressway back to Seoul, Soohyuk thought back to the fog over the lake that morning, and how the waters had glittered in the sun. Surrounding him were the sounds of other vehicles. In front, a big SUV turned on its signal lights and changed lanes. He glanced at the dashboard. 110 km/hr, fifty-two minutes until he reached home. Occasionally, the screen flashed red as the GPS system announced that speed enforcement cameras were a few hundred metres ahead.

The expressway stretching into the distance felt like a boundary; crossing it would leave behind the short respite and return him to the rhythm of daily life. In a while, he'd be going back to an empty house, eating his lunch alone again. A cold silence would still wrap around the well-organised space, where everything was placed in its rightful position. However, certain that something would be different this time, Soohyuk smiled.

6

FIRST SNOW, MISSING YOU, STORIES

Yoojin clicked on the folder [SOYANGRI BOOK KITCHEN_ PHOTOS] on her laptop. Ahead of the staff meeting tomorrow, she wanted to select the photos that would feature in the desk calendar they were designing for the new year.

The first photo she picked was of the warm spring sunshine streaming in through the large, spotless windows in the guesthouse living room. A night-sky photo that looked like it was taken in a different universe. Roses blooming in May, a beautiful mix of dark red and light pink petals among leaves of a brilliant green. The guests at the writers' studio deep in concentration while her employees wrote book-recommendation notes. She scrolled through photos of the sun setting behind the mountain ridges in late autumn, the back view of a couple browsing books at the café, a delicious breakfast spread of beef radish soup, stir-fried beef and egg rolls.

It was as if each photo also captured that particular day's temperature, humidity, the smell, the background music, the mood, her thoughts in that moment. There was a touch of melancholy, as though each photo was a moment frozen in time; when everything else had changed, they'd stay the same. It wasn't the dark or bleak kind of melancholy, but the kind of tender feeling knowing that all things would come to an end eventually, and at some point, you'd look back wistfully.

There were a couple of video clips too. Fireflies dancing in the garden on a midsummer night, a timelapse video capturing the dynamic changes in the sky, white fog passing by the valleys at dawn, voices of participants reading aloud in a book club meeting. In one of the clips, their go-to florist, Min, was in a work apron, potting plants in the garden as she chatted with Hyungjun.

Yoojin smiled as she watched the videos. Suddenly, she paused. In the video, two kids in rubber boots were having fun stepping on the chestnut burrs and on the edge of the frame was Soohyuk. He was in the baggy trousers Siwoo had lent him, smiling as the kids turned towards him. Just as one of them was about to trip, he quickly lent a hand. Her thoughts turned to his favourite jazz song.

After returning to Seoul, he never contacted them again. Not that they'd exchanged numbers, but if he'd wanted to, he could've dropped them a DM on Instagram. But instead of feeling disappointed or upset, she was more concerned about whether he was doing okay. The precarious look in his eyes would always be etched on her memory. She replayed the video several more times.

Yoojin looked up. The surroundings felt too quiet, as if the world was holding its breath. She looked out the window and realised it was snowing. The first snow of the year. Tiny snowflakes were lifted in a dance on the wind before spiralling downwards. The ground was covered with a thin layer of white; stepping on it lightly would form a clear, dark footprint. The insects and birds seemed to have gone quiet too, as the world was blanketed in silence.

Yoojin got up and pushed open the windows as far as they would go. It was as if everything was wearing a threadbare white cardigan. A soft sound like a broom sweeping the floor could be heard – the sound of falling snow.

In the book café, a Christmas song by Eddie Higgins Trio was flowing in the air. The same song she'd listened to with Sohee and Hyungjun on the night of the summer monsoon.

I wonder if everyone's well . . .

The faces swam up in her mind. Some she remembered in fine detail, others the shape of their lips as they spoke, the edge of their sweater, their dark brown hair dancing in the wind, their laughter.

Sometimes, the feeling of missing someone could get us through difficult moments, the comfort found in nostalgia and yearning. As she carried that feeling in her heart, perhaps it'd land gracefully like a snowflake on the person's shoulder and in that moment, they might be thinking of her too. Everyone was busy with their own lives, but when two people missed each other, it was as if a thread was connecting them, and as the rivulets of emotions deepened with the sense of longing, perhaps one day, they might find themselves converging again somewhere . . .

Yoojin, who'd been staring vacantly out the window, promptly stood up. Heading towards the book kitchen was a familiar face, looking stiff and awkward while leaving behind dark tracks in the now-covered road.

***

'I didn't think you'd really open a bookshop.'

The sunbae – her senior in school and later, ex-business partner – was trying to lighten the mood, but clearly it wasn't working. Yoojin pretended to be relaxed, but the stiffness in the corner of her lips said otherwise. On the opposite table were five middle-aged ladies having a mini class reunion. In contrast to their laughter and chatter, the silence between them felt even more uncomfortable.

'. . . Oh.'

He coughed awkwardly and sipped his milk tea. His looked around the book café, and his long, thin eyes made him seem unfriendly.

'You haven't been replying to my messages at all.'

'Well . . . I don't have anything to say.'

Sighing, he leaned back in the wooden chair, which creaked slightly under his weight.

'I asked to meet after you sold the company. I got Sanghyuk to pass on the message, and I tried to call you too, but you didn't pick up . . .'

A suffocating silence fell between them. Yoojin thought back to that night in the empty meeting room. In the darkness, she had stood like a statue as she fought back the tears. The silence pressed down on all sides, as if telling her, 'This is where it ends.'

That day, she'd had a huge fight with the sunbae over a proposal they'd received from a company that wanted to acquire their start-up. For the past three years, they'd hustled hard, and they were beginning to achieve some stability. They'd just raised a fresh round of venture capital and were celebrating the fact that they didn't have to worry about funds for at least the next year. Yoojin believed that it was a sign to take the company to even greater heights. Selling the company at this point was unthinkable. However, the sunbae had a different idea. He was a practical person. Knowing that

142

it was rare for a start-up to even reach its third anniversary, he thought that it'd be good for the start-up's growth, and their résumés, to sell it if a decent proposal came in.

'It's the best time to exit and maybe start something new. The terms are decent. We can even join their company if you want, and they'll be able to offer stock options as part of the buyout package.'

'But we just raised capital. What's the point of selling it and starting from scratch again?'

'Come on, we need to be objective. Which other company would value us at this amount? That we lasted three years is already a miracle. It'd take another ten years before the company can generate profits, but whether we'll last another three years is a question . . .'

'So you're trying to say that we should cash out when we can, and end things here?'

At her sharp words, his eyes grew colder. She stared resolutely back.

'Fine, Sunbae, if you want to leave, go. Whether it's to a venture capital firm, or to join that company, go ahead. Go be a serial start-up founder and bask in that title. I'm staying put.'

'Yoojin-ah . . .'

'How could you? Is that why you roped me into this in the first place? To use my consulting background to appeal to investors? What am I? A wrapping paper you discard when it's served its purpose?' Yoojin yelled.

'Yoojin, hear me out.'

'Hear you out? And then what? To listen to you, end things the way you want and live happily ever after? If you want to pull out so much, then go. Leave. Follow that grand plan you have for yourself. But don't force me to become the same kind of person.'

Their conversation was like a möbius strip, going in limbo, only the intensity was escalating, and the hurt deepening. In the end, he couldn't take it anymore. He packed up and left one day. They didn't sell the company then, but when Yoojin looked back, he had been right. He went on to do very well for himself at a venture capital firm, while her start-up was just drifting.

In the end, she sold their only asset – the patents – to a company for a decent offer, took the stock, and liquidated the company. He tried to contact her through classmates and the other seniors she was close to, but she shut him out. When everything was done and dusted, she didn't step out of her house for two months. All she wanted to do was be away from everyone and everything. She even seriously considered turning off her phone and going to the other side of the globe, whether it was Alaska or South America.

***

Siwoo, who had noticed the tension, quietly put down a plate of chocolate cookies, and nodded at her before disappearing behind the counter. At the next table, the ladies were still chatting loudly.

Yoojin broke the silence.

'. . . In the end, you're the more mature person. Thanks for coming all the way here to look for me.'

Yoojin looked closely at him. In the last three years, he seemed to have aged suddenly. Even though he was only in his mid-thirties, his hair was showing the first signs of greying, and there were wrinkles around his eyes. But he looked at home in his checked dark grey suit and polished leather shoes.

'Honestly . . . I was wondering if I'd come too late. When

I first heard that you'd opened this place, I thought it was so *you*. Do you still remember the first start-up idea we had? You were always interested in content curation – I remember you wanted to create a shop on the metaverse that would recommend music, books and movies according to the user's preferences. The passion for storytelling and content was always in you.'

Yoojin thought back to the days of spending summer nights at an open-air café, drinking beer and discussing start-up ideas with the sunbae. That was before she'd left her consultancy job, so they could only meet late at night at the café in front of her house, and their conversations often continued till the first light was out. They were thrilled about the adventures ahead, and she was brimming with courage and enthusiasm to tackle any obstacles that came her way. Start-ups were a 99 per cent failure, everyone said, but she was sure that with the sunbae, they could make it to the 1 per cent.

'You had many ideas, too. But honestly, what I really remember are the bottled beers we had and the snacks.'

The stiffness in his cheeks disappeared as he broke into a smile.

'I've been having reflux issues. I blame the cheese fries we inhaled at midnight.'

'Are you sure it wasn't the beers?' Yoojin quipped. 'Gosh, we could even have played Jenga with the bottle caps!'

They exchanged a smile. It had been fourteen years since they met as senior and junior classmen at the business school in university. He'd been the person who knew her the best in her twenties, perhaps even more so than her parents. She, too, had known him better than anyone else.

He was the kind of person who gave his all when he got interested in something. An obsessive, almost. When he got into snowboarding, he practised so much that he was bruised all over, and when he was studying for his chartered account-ant qualification, he turned off his phone all day, and only turned it back on for ten minutes to settle the most urgent stuff. When they were poring over the contracts, he'd look through every minute detail until the lawyer was fed up with his incessant questioning.

But here was the same sunbae sitting opposite her, looking like an old man alone at the beach reminiscing about the good old days of his youth. In the last three years as they had lived their thirties separately, a huge river now existed between them, an empty echo filling the gaps of time.

'. . . Do you remember? We almost named our company 'First Snow' and only gave up when we found out that another company was using it. But seeing the snow right now reminds me of that day.'

He took a white-chocolate cookie and stared out the window. The snow had become heavier, almost like a downpour. She glanced sideways at him and the memories came flooding back. Sunbae eating black-bean noodles with her at their faculty common room, Sunbae listening to her when she complained about her busy consulting life, Sunbae falling asleep on the sofa at the start-up when their meetings stretched into sunrise . . .

Everyone had their 'first snow' moments, or so Yoojin believed. Where the bustle of daily life quietened in an instant and changes came raining down like snowflakes. Only when the failures and the mess of the past were blanketed by the snow would the outline of life become clearer, just like how the edges of the fir trees become more pronounced in a white coat. In that moment, the painful times, the difficult periods that were seemingly hard to understand, turned into a meaningful landscape. And when those times came to pass, one would be able to gather the courage to snowboard from the snowcapped hill.

Siwoo and Serin went around the tables to light the candles. It was only five in the evening, but the sky was getting dark. The tiny flames and the bright snow outdoors enveloped Soyangri Book Kitchen.

'There's something I wanted to tell you,' Yoojin said. She avoided eye contact, but she could tell that he was looking at her with slightly raised eyebrows. His cheeks were stiff, and she remembered how his ears always reddened when he was flustered.

'. . . I'd occasionally think back to those days at the start-up. I was perpetually in a state of burnout. Although at that point, I hadn't realised.'

She paused to check his reaction, but he only looked at her calmly. Yoojin gazed at the flickering flame on the table.

'Back then, we were working eighty hours a week. We wanted success, we craved the acknowledgement of being good captains that could steer the ship well and deliver what we set out to do. Emotions were swept aside as we gave everything we had to the projects. We thought that was professionalism.'

Back then, she'd plunged deep into work, grasping on to her grand vision of being an explorer, a pioneer setting the way forward, not realising that her emotional state was broken like the aftermath of a battlefield. Feelings were always shoved on the back burner. Success had to come first. In her eyes, there were only goals, and nothing else.

'We were fighting every day, and come to think about it, I wasn't quite myself. Any minor thing could trigger my temper, and even though there wasn't anything to be *that* angry about,

I screamed at you all the time. And that day when we successfully raised capital . . . when I got home, I sat alone in the living room, feeling completely hollow on the inside. I'd achieved my goal, yet I felt nothing.'

Her voice shook as she thought back to those moments.

'Yoojin-ah . . .'

'I wanted to say sorry. For pinning all the blame on you, for calling you selfish, crass. Back then, I was so drained and worn out that I was just lashing out at everyone. I'm sorry I couldn't communicate my thoughts better.'

The words tumbled out of her. As the candle burned, the scent spiralled upwards, mixing with the smell of books in the air.

'Me too,' he said calmly.

Yoojin looked up and saw that he was smiling.

'We were drowning back then. Our lives were consumed by work, yet we basked in pride that we'd made work our hobby. We were blind to the fact that we were burned out. I'm sorry. Sorry for not being a supportive pillar as a sunbae should. Instead, I was struggling myself,' he said, gazing at her intensely.

For a moment, Yoojin thought she was seeing the younger sunbae from university days before they had embarked on the start-up. She'd first met him at the school's entrepreneurship club. Back then, he was fun to hang out with. They clicked well with each other and he always managed to make her laugh.

'Actually, I've got something to discuss with you,' he added.

Nervousness flashed in her eyes as she sat a little straighter, but he was smiling brightly at her.

'The company I'm with now is keen to create a private library for its employees and they're looking for someone to curate the books. It's a tech company, so they want books about entrepreneurship and creative content, and because there'll be times our work can get intense, they thought it'd be nice to have a collection of healing reads too. Isn't this the perfect project for you? I'm not asking you to give me the answer now, but I hope you'll consider it.'

The sunbae placed his name card on the table. *Director of Strategy Planning*. Yoojin picked up the card and smiled.

'Wow, a director. Since it's a request from you, Sunbae, what's there to think about? But how much are you offering? Also, is it a one-off curation service? Or would you refresh the collection with a different theme? I suppose the first theme is already decided – creativity and burnout.'

They laughed.

'As expected of Jung Yoojin! I can always count on you to jump straight into action. I take it that you're saying yes? In that case, drop by our Seoul office sometime next month. I'll introduce you to the staff member who's handling the project and they can answer all your questions. Oh, right. We'll need a name for the library.'

Yoojin nodded as she quickly made a memo on her phone. For a moment, he watched her in silence.

'Why did you call this place 'Soyangri Book Kitchen'? Soyangri – this, I get. But 'book kitchen'? At first, I thought you were running some kind of restaurant.'

'You're not the only one. I've had queries on cooking classes, and someone even misread *kitchen* as *chicken* and called to order fried chicken.'

The sunbae slapped his knees and roared in laughter.

'Book Chicken. Rolls off the tongue perfectly.'

'Hey!' Yoojin protested as she laughed. Through the long windows, the landscape looked like an ink-and-wash painting.

'It's as its name suggests. A kitchen of books to fill the emptiness of the heart, just like food fills our stomach. There're many others who remind me of the old me – burned out but unaware. I hope that they'll be able to fill their starving hearts with stories. Even better if they can learn to write about their feelings.'

'I see . . . so that's why you have a book café and rooms for a book-themed stay,' he murmured, nodding.

The clink of cutlery from the next table was like music in the background. Outside, the sky was the colour of dark roast coffee, making the candle flames seem even more luminous. But even without the candles, the snow brightened up the surroundings.

'. . . Yoojin, you're looking much better these days,' said the sunbae, looking more relaxed himself. 'I mean it . . . It's as if you've grown stronger, comfortable with being truly yourself.'

Yoojin saw him to his car before returning to the café. Through the windows, she could make out the footprints. Because the snow was thicker now, instead of black tracks, it was a series of white prints – the big ones by the sunbae, and her smaller sneaker prints next to them.

Standing by the window, she took out his name card again. The small, stiff card seemed to fill the gap of the past three years. It seemed like a lifetime ago that she was handing out her name cards stamped with the logo of the start-up, yet it also felt as though it was only yesterday.

The snow was getting heavier. The book café was relatively empty. Suddenly, the door opened, and a rush of cold air swept in, along with a few snowflakes.

'Yoojin nuna, have you heard? Diane is releasing her new album today!' Siwoo exclaimed as he hurried inside.

'Of course. You've been repeating that three times a day for the past week.'

'Oh yeah, and she's going live on the radio at seven. Wait. Oh my God. It's already eleven minutes past seven! Nooo, how could I not realise? I set an alarm too!'

Siwoo quickly settled down next to Yoojin and opened the radio app on his phone. Diane and the radio presenter appeared on the screen. The female presenter was speaking.

'Today is first of December. We welcomed our first snow of the year, and right now we have the most exciting gift from the queen who's back with a regular album after four years. Let's welcome Diane!'

'Hello, this is Diane. It's been a long time since I last greeted everyone with new music. Thank you for having me on the show.'

'Aww. The mood at our recording studio now is so warm and cosy. Everyone, from the staff to our PD, is grinning from ear to ear. We've just listened to the title song from the album – "What We Love in Winter". What a fresh, lovely song! Can you tell us more about the song, Diane?'

'Sure. It's a tribute to the years of being a singer-songwriter. I wrote it thinking back to the warm memories that shone through even in difficult times and the people who have been a strong pillar of support.'

'In just an hour, it's already charting at number one on major music charts. We expect no less from Diane. Congratulations!'

'Thank you. We just welcomed the first snow of the season, and that probably adds to the vibes of the song. Thank you for listening! Special thanks to the amazing staff and the producers who worked hard on the album.'

'I'm curious. Out of the songs on this album, which one carries the deepest meaning for you? We'd love to hear more!'

'There's a song that fills me with longing each time I listen to it. The last instrumental track – "Grandma and the Night Sky". My grandma passed away four years ago. She was a very special person to me and I wrote this song as a letter to her.'

'I believe this is your first self-composed instrumental track, right? Without further ado, let's listen to it right now.'

The track began with a piano solo. Yoojin pictured a gentle breeze blowing while taking a stroll on a narrow walking path. Gradually, the tempo and the intensity increased, as though waves were hitting the shore. Deep cello notes joined in the piano melody, and Yoojin thought of bright stars twinkling in the dark sky. She liked how the viola added to the depth of the emotions and as the song came to an end with the familiar melody from the start – this time, a cello solo – Yoojin thought of the autumn winds at Soyangri.

There wasn't any dramatic climax, nor was there an intentional hook. Da-in simply put in her memories and feelings – the moments of stargazing at night with her grandmother, the heart flutters she'd felt seeing the shining stars. It was a simple track, yet the emotions shone through, like a sincere handwritten letter.

That night, Yoojin mulled over what Da-in had told her.

Sometimes, I dream of Grandma's place. The sun's always out, and Grandma is there in her beautiful hanbok, smiling without a word. I catch a whiff of the chestnut trees from my childhood, and I'm there watching the world coloured in hues of purple and red.

Outside, the plum blossom trees stood in silence, the boughs arched as if craning to hear the music inside. Snowflakes settled on the branches and as the night deepened, it became a layer of white, like the shaved ice in patbingsu.

Winter had arrived with the first snow, but it didn't feel

cold at all. Was it because of the lingering warmth of the guests and customers? The courage of those who braved the snowy mountain roads to get here? Or the soothing piano instrumental track? Yoojin looked out at the snow sitting on the branches. For a moment, it was as if the sea of stars she'd seen with Da-in had descended upon the landscape before her eyes.

7

BECAUSE IT'S CHRISTMAS

Jihoon had not stirred an inch in the past hour. Today was Christmas Eve, and the café was at its busiest. He'd come in at around three, and without saying anything, had ordered a hot Americano. Serin greeted him enthusiastically, but he returned the greeting weakly. The light in his eyes had been extinguished.

After getting his coffee, Jihoon made his way to the picnic table in the back garden. He sat completely still, like a small creature crouched in a dark tunnel, lost. The biting winter winds were making his sleeves flap loudly, but he didn't even touch the hot drink. Soon, snow started falling.

'Serin, isn't that the . . . firefly guy? I've never met anyone more romantic.'

Siwoo had come up behind Serin as she stared out at Jihoon. She nodded.

'That evening, after the wedding ceremony, the two of them sat in the book café for quite a while before leaving separately. I had no idea what happened. I'm dying to know . . .'

'Isn't he your friend or something? Just text him.'

'Oh please. Only you would do that. I'm not that bold to ask him directly.'

Siwoo nodded absentmindedly as he put away the bag of

chocolate chips for cookies, together with the ingredients for lemon cake.

Jihoon was still in the same position, looking as if he'd lost his ability to speak, as if trying to will himself to forget everything. The falling snowflakes mixed with the rain, and as dusk fell, the sleet was getting heavier.

He thought back to the night of the fireflies and what Mari had said.

Jihoon-ah, do you know what I like about being with you? It's that I don't have to lie. How I score in exams is never important; you won't pry into my family affairs; and I don't have to entertain questions about my new bag or shoes. With you by my side . . . I can simply be myself. I have a lot of secrets, but I wasn't a bad kid. But after leaving you, I feel as if I've been destroying myself . . .

Jihoon could sense where the conversation was going, and why she'd brought this up. While her expression was more relaxed now, he found himself stiffening in anxiety.

I started out with small untruths. But by the time I realised it, my qualifications, résumé, my family – everything about me had become a lie. Or rather, I had come to believe that as real. So when an eligible bachelor proposed to me, I didn't think twice before saying yes. Now that I think back, I probably saw it as an opportunity to climb the social ladder. Now the person I call my husband is suing me. It's been a year, but this fight is dragging out. The visit to Korea is a brief respite for me. Here, I can breathe a little easier. Maybe because it's my birthplace after all . . .

What Mari didn't say was that she'd come back to meet him. She didn't want to admit that she'd hoped to see him once more in this lifetime. On the plane, she'd thought that if she could see him just once more, she'd be able to die in peace.

Now that she had, she didn't think it necessary to tell him that he'd given her the courage to keep going.

Jihoon, I'll accept the gift . . . and I hope that you'll remember me in the same way that you might an old diary that you'd flip through occasionally.

Mari, I . . .

Let me stay as a distant memory in your life. I'm not the person for you, whether it's now, or in the future.

Mari's tone was firm.

Behind the picnic table, snow was landing silently on the plum blossom branches. Jihoon looked past the backyard, as if hoping to see someone approaching from the forest. Serin followed his gaze. He looked so forlorn, like the ending scene of a melancholic movie. Christmas carols were playing from the speakers at the book café, but she wasn't in the festive mood at all.

Serin hesitated. She watched Jihoon let his coffee go cold. Was it okay to meddle in his affairs? she wondered. Her thoughts drifted to Mari, who'd returned alone to the book kitchen for the second time just as summer was ending, and she looked over to the drawer below the counter.

***

About ten days after that night with the fireflies, Mari came back to Soyangri Book Kitchen. It was almost six in the evening, when the café was about to close, but the humid weather dug its heels in. In the distance, heavy grey rainclouds hung low. It was the kind of evening where a thunderstorm could begin at any moment.

Serin immediately recognised the woman who cautiously

opened the door and stepped inside. If it was Siwoo, he'd have greeted her affably, but the best Serin could do was to stop herself from looking too surprised. Mari looked thinner than the last time she'd seen her. Serin quickly saved the file of the brochure she was working on and stood up. She flashed a bright smile at Mari.

'Good to see you again! You're Jihoon's friend, right?'

Mari nodded politely in greeting. 'Oh, I didn't think you'd remember me.' Even in a simple white T-shirt and jeans, she exuded elegance. Pausing for a second, Mari seemed to be gathering courage for what she was about to say.

'. . . Is the letter-writing event still ongoing by any chance?'

That was the activity the book café had run in the month of April, where customers could write a letter to themselves, and the staff would mail it out at Christmas together with the book of their choice. The reception had been great, and months later, they still received enquiries every now and then.

Serin smiled. 'Not officially, but since you're Jihoon's friend, I'll be happy to accommodate.'

Mari returned the smile. Serin was reminded of the perfect, professional smile of a department-store employee. From the moment Mari mentioned letters, Serin's instinct as a romance-drama fanatic had kicked in. *She must be hoping to leave something for Jihoon.* Realising that she was now playing a side character in their story, Serin's heart pounded wildly as she bobbed her head.

'This . . .' Mari murmured, taking out a book from her tote bag.

Through the translucent plastic wrapper, Serin could make out the title and the yellow butterfly illustration on the cover. It was Kaori Ekuni's picture book *Butterfly*. And on the wrapper, Mari had written: *To my dear friend, Jihoon*

'Would it be possible to request the book be delivered next year? 31 July to be exact – on his birthday. By then . . . I'll have left Korea . . . You can put the sender as Soyangri Book Kitchen.'

Mari gave her Jihoon's address and contact details, before ordering an iced café latte to go. When she walked out, her shoulders were visibly relaxed, as if relieved at having completed a difficult task.

***

Mari's profile morphed into Jihoon's as Serin pulled her thoughts back to reality. Mari had told her to mail out the book next summer, so she couldn't break her promise and give it to him today. But she wondered if she ought to drop a hint. There were times in life where a flicker of hope could keep one going.

After a moment's hesitation, Serin started making a cup of hot chocolate. She added only half the usual amount of whipped cream. Jihoon didn't look like he had a sweet tooth. She dusted some cinnamon powder on top and on a small white oval dish, she placed a small walnut cookie. The contrasting colours made the drink resemble a little wooden hut hidden deep in the forest. She walked slowly, careful not to spill the drink.

The snow was getting heavier, and the wind howled in bursts, like a washing machine in its spin-dry cycle. Serin turned out to the back garden. The first thing she noticed was the snow resting on the plum blossom branches.

Jihoon was nowhere to be seen. There was a dark outline on the snow-covered bench; he must've just left. Serin set down the tray and held up the mug. A sweet aroma tickled her nose as the warmth spread to her fingers. She looked at the narrow path ahead. It was as though she could still see the fireflies in the midsummer night.

Serin thought about the picture book that'd reach Jihoon next summer. What was Mari trying to tell him? Which sentence would speak to him the most? Serin remembered a line from the book.

A butterfly can go anywhere. Flitting
from yesterday to today.

***

It was about one o'clock in the afternoon on Christmas Eve when Nayoon returned to her studio apartment and noticed the package by her door. On this day, most people had either taken leave or were working a half-day. Her office didn't have strict working hours; this morning, the office was practically deserted. She'd ordered a cranberry chicken sandwich from a nearby café and eaten at her desk as she checked her inbox, which was quiet. At 12.33 p.m., she had left the office.

Nayoon was supposed to have dinner at her elder brother's house at five. She couldn't wait to see her little princess – her niece, Chae-eun – who was at the age where she was speaking super cutely despite mispronouncing words at times. Her brother laughed and said that his daughter was counting down to Aunt Nayoon's visit, even more so than Santa Claus's, because she had promised to come with a *Frozen* Elsa dress. In their family group chat there was a video of Chae-eun dancing to 'Santa Claus is Coming to Town'. Nayoon's heart melted at her dimples.

The moment she got home, she tore open the package.

Inside was a bubble-wrapped copy of *Tsubaki Stationery Store*, and her sealed letter to herself. There was also a Polaroid photo of falling cherry blossom petals against the backdrop of Soyangri Book Kitchen, and the glint of the warm sunlight. Nayoon could almost feel the wind that day. Soft and fluffy, like cotton candy.

That spring day she'd spent at the book kitchen felt like aeons ago. It was only three turns of seasons, yet it felt as though she'd dived into a different world and returned through the revolving doors.

What was it like for Serin, whose daily life was now Soyangri Book Kitchen? On the rare occasions they spoke, she always sounded excited and busy over the phone, as if a different wind was blowing at her end. She'd not gone to Namwoo's wedding, of course. But Nayoon couldn't quite tell if her friend was pretending to be upbeat, or if the book kitchen had changed her, or whether she'd always been like this.

Nayoon broke the seal and opened the letter, thinking that she'd still remember what she wrote. But she was wrong. The Nayoon who'd written the letter that day was completely different from Nayoon today. All she could recall was the touch of the pen nib on the paper.

Dear Nayoon,

Merry Christmas! It must be Christmas Eve when you're reading this, but right now I'm still living in the season of cherry blossoms. The weather's warming up, so we don't even need a trench coat when riding our bicycles.

This is the first time I've written a letter to myself. Am I even making sense? I don't know, but I thought I'd write this how I'd write in a diary and let my thoughts just be all over the place. How are you doing? Yesterday, I came here with Chanwook and Serin and we were scream-singing to 'Cherry Blossom Ending' on a Friday night. I felt so much lighter, but the next moment, I felt sad. Why sad, you may ask? I think it's because I realised I rarely check in on myself or reflect on my feelings.

Anyway . . . I choked up at the sight of the cherry blossoms in full bloom and the petals being carried in the wind. It's like the song title . . . my twenties were ending . . . I can't help but think like this. Will I ever achieve anything if life continues on this trajectory? Will I get married and how so? I'm already twenty-nine, but I still can't see where my life is heading. By the time Christmas Eve comes around, will I have figured out my feelings? Or will I forget all about everything and go to work with my usual blank look?

Yours,
Nayoon from April

There was a surprise in the package – a postcard. Written at the top in a neat hand was: *A Christmas Eve Invitation*. Below was an illustration of a shopfront, the signboard above with the words *Prescribing the Recipe Book of Your Life*. Looking into the window, several children were decorating a Christmas tree inside the shop.
Nayoon flipped to the back.

Join us for a Christmas Eve party at Soyangri Book Kitchen! Bring a favourite book or a comforting read for a book exchange. The remaining books will be donated to Soyang

*Elementary School, so feel free to bring a stack! And if you
don't have a book, it's okay. Why? Because it's Christmas.*

Below were further handwritten details on the gathering.
She recognised Serin's writing. And when she got to the P.S.,
she chuckled.

P.S. Nayoon-ah. Time to leave the house now!

Some days were like this invitation – an unexpected curve-
ball to a day that was going according to plan. Should she still
have dinner with her brother's family? Or should she make an
impromptu trip to the book kitchen?

In a small caramel purse, she slipped in her phone, a mini
notebook and a Lamy fountain pen. Then she grabbed a
grey padded coat – her thickest – from her closet and called
her brother to see if she could come by tomorrow morning
instead. It would be really special to see Chae-eun's excitement
on Christmas morning. It was two in the afternoon. Outside,
thick grey clouds hung low in the sky, making it look as if it
was already evening.

***

Dusk was falling over Soyangri Book Kitchen. It was snowing
heavily. When Nayoon and Chanwook entered the garden,
they caught sight of the plum blossom trees. With Christmas lights twined around the bark, they'd transformed into
Christmas trees. A small crowd had gathered, writing notes
and letters to be put in time capsules. Their gaze landed on
the banner hung across the small takeout café stand.

WELCOME TO SOYANGRI BOOK KITCHEN

One. Recommend a book that brings out the flavours of life, be it the bitterness, sweetness, saltiness, spiciness or the umami.

Two. Participate in the time capsule letter-writing activity. We'll open them together, same time next year.

Three. Feel free to take a book from the donation table. One per person!

Through the large windows, Nayoon and Chanwook caught a glimpse of the interior and their eyes widened in surprise.

'Wow, a completely different vibe!'

'It's winter outside, but inside, it's as if summer has returned . . . a midsummer Christmas?'

Pushing the door open, they were greeted by the glittering lights on the palm tree masquerading as a Christmas tree. From the sangria table, they could hear the tinkle of ice cubes in glasses; a bottle of Moscato was being chilled in the ice bucket. Next to a basket of bright yellow lemons was a note indicating that these were the ingredients to make lemon cake.

'Nayoooooooon!'

'Ah! Seriiiiiin!' Nayoon exclaimed, mimicking her tone.

Serin came bouncing over like an excited puppy and threw herself into Nayoon's embrace. The two ladies, who were about the same height, held each other's shoulders and danced around like in a ganggangsullae traditional dance.

'Oooh, Yi Chanwook! I see you've put in some extra effort today,' Serin exclaimed, eyeing Chanwook's outfit.

'He went for a blind date today, but he got dumped even before they met,' Nayoon said, chuckling.

'Blind date?'

'Yeah, when else have you ever seen him dressed up like this?'

'Come on, Choi Nayoon. I wasn't dumped, she asked to meet on the twenty-sixth instead.'

'Isn't that the same thing?'

As they laughed and chatted, Nayoon discreetly observed Serin. In just six months, something about her had changed. First, her skin was slightly tanned, and her jawline was more pronounced.

'Serin, have you lost weight? You look a little different.'

'Really? We don't have any scales here, so I can't tell. But I'm practically on my feet the entire day – opening cartons of books, tending to the garden, preparing meals. I guess I'm forced to exercise, heh.'

In Serin's words, life in Soyangri was always busy and hectic, yet Nayoon could feel the calm vibes emanating off her.

'Where's Siwoo?'

'He'll be stuck in the kitchen for a while. We're cooking quite a few dishes. I'll let him know that you guys are here. He'll probably want to pop out to say hi,' Serin said as she craned her neck towards the kitchen.

Noticing that, Chanwook wriggled his eyebrows.

'Aigoo, don't you guys look like husband and wife owners of the guesthouse?'

Nayoon burst out laughing. She was just thinking the same. Serin shook her head; it was so absurd that it wasn't even worth retorting.

'Well, if sparks are going to fly, the fireworks would've started ten years ago.'

'Romance doesn't follow logic. Who knows? When you realise it, you might have an entire fireworks display!' Nayoon teased.

'Guys? *Wake up.* Get some food and find your common sense. I'll leave you two here; I still have things to do. You two are staying the night, got it?'

Serin didn't even wait for an answer before leaving to speak to another member of staff. It was a hive of activity at the book kitchen.

Nayoon and Chanwook made their way to the buffet table. Nayoon helped herself to some Korean braised beef short ribs, smoked salmon salad and fries, and returned to her seat with a cup of coffee. Chanwook, on the other hand, was still standing there, his gaze fixed on something to the right of the table.

'Wait . . . that looks familiar?'

Nayoon turned to see what Chanwook was staring at. It was the shelf that displayed Soyangri Book Kitchen's own merchandise. There was a notebook with an illustration of three Pomeranian puppies running in the garden at Soyangri Book Kitchen. There were also postcards and recyclable totes printed with the illustrations of a couple sitting at the book café and an elderly couple browsing the shelves with a smile.

'Oh, Serin did those,' said Siwoo, who'd appeared by her side.

Nayoon's eyes rounded. 'Really?'

Siwoo smiled, nodding.

Chanwook whistled. 'Wow, Min Serin!'

Nayoon and Chanwook went up for a closer look. Then, at the same time, they turned in the direction of Serin. Noticing them staring, she waved her hands above her head enthusiastically, grinning. Just like that spring day in April.

She walked towards them, carrying a mug of hot chocolate. She blew on the steam carefully and when she spoke, her tone was nonchalant.

'The illustrations were meant for our social media marketing, but everyone loved them, so we ended up incorporating them into the merch. We're planning to open an online shop next year.'

Nayoon looked impressed.

'You're amazing. I must get your autograph now before you become too famous. But seriously, we barely hear from you these days. Is life that great here?'

'If it is, you bet I'll be calling you every day to boast. There's really nothing much to do in the countryside. It's a bit embarrassing to be complaining about being lonely, so I chose to focus on my work.'

'Min Serin, you're breaking my heart. Please, we have so many fun activities!' Siwoo pretended to be miffed.

'See what I mean? People are going to think there's *something* going on between the both of you,' Nayoon quipped.

Serin rolled her eyes. 'We're partners in crime.'

'. . . That's what people call their lovers,' Chanwook sniggered.

Serin and Siwoo looked on in exasperation as Nayoon and Chanwook broke out in peals of laughter.

The four of them sat at a table by the window and looked out to the garden. It was snowing lightly, and a young child was dancing around like a puppy seeing snow for the first time. Over a purple velvet dress, she wore a checked coat, and with her cheeks flushed, she looked like a tiny Christmas tree. Turning to her mother, the little girl spun round several times as if to show off her outfit, grinning. Her plaits danced like tiny waves. Nayoon was reminded of her niece, Chae-eun.

'Honestly, I can't imagine having kids myself,' she said.

'I know what you mean. The kids who come here are so cute, but their meltdowns scare me. And those who stick to their mums like gum; she can't even leave the kids for a moment, even for a toilet break. I can't imagine it happening to me,' said Serin.

Chanwook crossed his arms and leaned back.

'Well, it's not just about kids. I can't even imagine getting married. That feels like something in the distant future.'

'Same,' Siwoo said as he gulped down the sangria. 'Like it'll be another two hundred years before marriage or kids are on the horizon.'

A wan smile tugged at Nayoon's lips as she nodded. A calm waltz song was playing in the background, a fitting track for the opening scene of a movie. The start of a new story, a new chapter.

'Ooh I love this song. Yoojin Sajangnim puts it on every day. Guys, listen to it.'

The four of them fell silent as they let the melody wash over them. The song was 'Waltz for Debby', about a little girl dancing to silent music who'd grow up in the blink of an eye. Darkness had fallen, and in the garden, the plum blossom trees stood brightly, and the lighting from the small café stand looked like stage lights shining on the little girl and her mother. It was as if they were watching a musical.

Nayoon thought about her niece. In a flash, five-year old Chae-eun would be no more, as she turned six, seven, eight . . . By the time Chae-eun celebrated her twentieth birthday, the five-year-old Chae-eun would only exist in photos and videos. Twenty-year-old Chae-eun would likely be a university student. She wouldn't remember how she'd tried to eat snow, the times she'd stumbled cutely over her words. The memories would only be carried by those who'd watched her grow up, like film that hadn't been developed. Nayoon felt a tight squeeze in her throat.

Serin was still watching the little girl.

'I guess we were once her age. Why is it that we don't remember our childhood?'

Chanwook stretched, lifting his arms high as he turned his gaze away from the child.

'I know, right. If God exists, why did He make humans this way? Why make us forget? It's like we have amnesia.'

'Maybe God loves time capsules?' Nayoon blurted out her thoughts.

'Huh?'

The three of them stared at her.

'Think about it. Doesn't it feel as though we're opening a time capsule by the time we turn thirty – a letter that our parents buried in their hearts when we were five. They remember all the moments that we don't – all those times where we were just beginning to explore the world around us, so clueless but lovable. The times of waking up at three in the morning to change our nappies, cooing at us in baby-speak, and when we cried at a balloon bursting, they'd soothe us. And the teddy bear I used to play with, they'd probably still remember it. And when years have passed and it's time for us to be parents ourselves, we finally start to understand how our parents felt. Isn't that like opening a time capsule?'

Serin nodded, her hands still wrapped around her mug.

'Many guests here come with their families. Sometimes I'll see them fighting, sometimes teasing each other, and I find myself thinking that all these moments are an accumulation of the love they have for each other. What does it mean to be human? Perhaps it's the moments of loving someone and being loved that keep us going in life.'

'. . . *Moments of loving someone and being loved that keep us going in life*. Wow, Min Serin. You've become quite the poet,' Chanwook laughed, ruffling her hair.

It was as if in that instant, the road ahead had cleared up for Nayoon. What truly mattered wasn't whether to open a macaron dessert shop or to stay in her office job. It was the realisation that each and every one of us is an imperfect being made with love. Me, you, everyone else. The warmth to melt the ice beneath our feet as we walk through the depths of winter, the courage to keep going despite criticisms, the resilience to pull through the seemingly never-ending failures and rejections – it was all possible because of moments of loving and being loved. Humans might be imperfect, but love was perfect.

Christmas carols, along with the laughter and chatter of guests, filled the air at Soyangri Book Kitchen. Outside, the little girl was now making the snowman's carrot nose with her dad.

***

Sohee parked the car and turned off the engine. Before getting out, she checked herself in the mirror. Her silver earrings stood out against the black turtleneck she was wearing. She paused to steady her breathing. With a thud, she closed the door. The side mirror folded automatically with a *znnnng*, and somehow it felt like an encouragement, telling her that everything would be fine.

With small careful steps, Sohee walked across the

snow-covered car park to the garden. It was nighttime, but the bustle of activity felt as though a second sun had risen at night. Along the path were two tiny snowmen and she was delighted to see the plum blossoms lit up like Christmas trees. Against the white snow, red camellias by the path shone like rubies. Sohee, too, was wearing a pair of floral earrings today. A soft smile appeared on her lips and that moment, her black turtleneck didn't feel so suffocating anymore. Taking a deep breath, she headed towards the book café.

Back when Sohee was discharged from the hospital, the weather had been the complete opposite. In August, the summer flowers were in full bloom. After completing the discharge procedures, she had made her way home amid the loud cries of cicadas. Even when the windows were closed, she could still hear them screaming outside, as if urging her to return to the hustle and bustle of daily life.

By the time she had woken up from her nap that day, it was already seven in the evening, yet it was still bright outside. The summer heat lingered in the air. Sohee had changed into a sleeveless turtleneck and gone for a walk. To her, the turtleneck was a 'sign' of sorts, marking the ending of a chapter in her life. She was saying goodbye to thyroid cancer. Between her neck and her chest was a crescent-shaped scar from the surgery. The turtleneck had quietly covered the mark, yet her closet of turtlenecks was a stark reminder of the times she had spent in the hospital.

The silver earrings Sohee was wearing this evening had been an impulse buy, from a truck vendor by the road when she was out for an evening walk. When she had first seen them in the glow of a midsummer sunset, they looked like two flowers blooming in the desert. There was a round pearl in the middle, and the ends of the petals were slightly bent, making them look even more real.

Putting on the earrings tonight made her feel like a different person. Like the turtleneck, it was also a sign – not to hide, but to be displayed. It was the sign that she'd managed to return to the summer of life from the clutches of death in a cold operating theatre. But it was only now, as she stared at the flowers in the snow, that she realised her earrings were in the shape of a camellia. I made the right decision coming here, she thought.

'Goodness! Sohee-ssi! I thought you weren't able to make it,' Yoojin exclaimed as she ran towards her. Having drunk a glass of sangria, she gave off a light scent of red wine.

The atmosphere in the book café was different from how she'd remembered last summer. Chatter and laughter permeated the air, with the occasional clink of plates and cutlery. Surrounded by a delicious aroma, her nervousness eased. She thought back to the food she'd eaten during her last visit – a hearty beef radish stew, seasoned soybean paste bibimbap, aged kimchi stew with pork. She remembered how she'd jolt awake in the middle of the night, overwhelmed by fear of her upcoming surgery. But the next moment, her thoughts turned to the warm breakfast that would await her the next morning, the homestyle cooking that she loved so much. Wondering which dishes would be served for breakfast, she drifted back to sleep.

'Sorry I'm late! How've you been?' A soft smile lit up her face. Finally. She'd waited for this moment for a long time. And in her eyes, she added:

I missed this place, even though it came with memories of fear and heavy feelings.

Yoojin, face slightly flushed from the drinks, pulled Sohee to a seat before plonking down in the chair beside her. She needed to sit and look at Sohee properly. She wanted to ask her if she was alright, if she'd recovered fully, but she stopped herself. Putting herself in Sohee's shoes, it wasn't as if everything would end just because the surgery went well. She'd need some time to heal, not just physically. Instead, Yoojin nodded at her and pushed a big ceramic plate into her hands. Sohee felt the weight in her palms.

'Here! Have your dinner first. You must be tired from the drive.'

Yoojin raised her voice slightly so that it wouldn't be drowned out by the music and the noise. She sounded more excitable than usual. Sohee thought back to the day of the jazz music festival, where she'd cheered hard and even high-fived strangers. Memories of being in a raincoat, surrounded by the smells of grass and plants, swaying her body to the rhythm, the way everyone was reluctant to leave even when night had fallen, enjoying a late-night chat with Hyungjun and Yoojin at the book café. Everything was coming back to her.

'I'm starving. Can't wait to see what our chef has prepared for us.'

With a bright smile, Sohee held out a bulging paper bag to Yoojin.

'Ooh, are these the books? Wow, how many did you bring?'

'Since you said the remaining books would be donated, I brought quite a few,' said Sohee, grinning.

Yoojin's dimples deepened as she peered into the bag. Her gaze landed on something and she looked up in surprise.

'What's this?'

It was a square book and being larger than the rest, it had

caught her attention. At first, Yoojin wondered if it was a photo album, but looking at the quality of the paper, it didn't seem so. The cover was wrapped in velvet and in the middle was what looked like a big round mirror, decorated with gold lace around it. This was clearly a handmade book.

Now that she took a closer look, she realised it wasn't a mirror. Inside the gold-laced oval shape was an illustration of a girl sitting on a rooftop, admiring the moon. There was a small chimney, which was painted brick-red and gold. She peered closely and saw gold-dust powder. It was as if the moon on the top left was also gazing down at the girl. The shape wasn't perfect; a full moon missing a sliver. The girl's expression wasn't drawn clearly, but from her relaxed pose, the tilt of her head, it looked like she was at ease. The book was bound with a patterned rope in Christmas red and green, looped across its top right and bottom left corners. On the top right corner was a lovely pink ribbon that was perfect for a five-year-old child.

'It's . . . my first fairy tale book.'

Yoojin's eyes widened. Feeling embarrassed, Sohee hurriedly explained, 'It's not made for sale. I wanted a keepsake to remember the month-long stay here, a present for myself. I came here hoping to read as much as I could and keep a diary. Do you remember that night when it was raining cats and dogs? After that night, it was as if I could hear a child's voice in me, asking if I wanted to go on an adventure.'

Sohee remembered how the summer sun had shone through the window at the writers' studio. That was the first day she wrote about Sophia.

'The child's name is Sophia. She's a witch who works at the Moonlight Bookshop and her dream is to become a guardian of books. The witches and wizards who visit the bookshop regale her with stories of the mysterious magical worlds near and far, and part of her work involves travelling through space and time to unfamiliar places to curate books on magic. She is able to teleport anywhere on a full-moon night as long as she returns within twenty-four hours. Because she can be quite absentminded, she hasn't received her certification to be a magical guardian of books. One day, on a full-moon night just before Christmas, a thief sneaks in, and she returns from her journey to discover that all the magical books to be delivered as presents at Christmas are gone. As for how the story ends, I'll leave you to read it, haha.'

'Wow. This sounds amazing!'

Yoojin pulled the book close to her chest. Because she could feel the tears swirling in her eyes, she quickly looked up at the ceiling before leaning forward to hug Sohee. Some emotions didn't need words to be expressed. A beating heart, a sincere look, was enough. Sohee could feel the unspoken in Yoojin's hug. She was never one who teared up easily, but her scar on her chest tingled, as if something was threatening to spill over. Sohee patted Yoojin's back gently.

Laughing, she teased, 'How can you be so touched when you haven't even read the story?'

'Oh yeah. Maybe I should've gone easy on the wine?' Yoojin smiled even as the tears continued to swirl in her eyes.

'Let It Snow' by Eddie Higgins Trio played in the background as laughter rang out from the next table. Smiling, Sohee went to the buffet table and helped herself to potato gratin and cheese kimbap. Yoojin loosened the rope binding and taking care not to let the ribbon fall off, she flipped open the thick, stiff paper.

PROLOGUE

Sophia remembers everything that happened in Moonlight Bookshop during the summer she turned five. It was a full-moon night. Someone walked in. At the tinkle of the bell, Sophia looked up.

Right at that moment, on the cramped shelves, a book appeared out of nowhere. It was covered with a layer of dust, as if it had been there forever. Sophia blinked. She stared at the book innocently lying there when her eyes suddenly widened. The book that was glowing just a moment ago had dimmed and vanished! It was just three short seconds, but because the shelf was at her eye level, she'd been staring at it without blinking. Wait! There it was again. It had returned.

A customer who'd been loitering at the bookshop for quite a while picked up the book and decided to buy it. That night, Sophia tried telling her mum what she'd witnessed, but her mum had no idea what she was talking about.

The secret was only to be revealed twenty-five years later.

'That was my mistake.'

Alice, who was a little older than Sophia and also an aspiring guardian of books back then, spoke calmly, but the look in her eyes held a shadow. That customer was destined to meet the book of their life that day, so the Association of Wizardry had placed a reservation spell for it to appear right on the dot. But Alice had accidentally muttered a vanishing spell instead. Luckily, her mentor Harriet caught her mistake and quickly reversed the spell.

Because Alice was only nine, the association decided not to pursue the matter, but that was only the beginning of her series of mistakes . . .

'This sounds fun,' said Hyungjun, who had appeared at their table. Sohee turned and smiled at him. 'When did you make this? Ms Attorney, aren't you having a little too much free time?' he teased good-naturedly.

'It has become my hobby. I spend the bulk of my day burying my nose in formal documents, so in my own free time, I want to write something light-hearted and sweet.'

Hyungjun took the seat next to Sohee and was about to say something when Siwoo appeared like a flash of lightning.

'Oh my God! Isn't this Ms Choi? It's been a long while.'

'Wait, you remember me? You have a great memory.'

Sohee liked how he was always his cheery self. Back in summer when she was withering, his bubbly voice was like a carbonated drink.

Siwoo chuckled. 'Of course! How could I forget a guest who has stayed with us for a whole month? And aren't you the one featured in Hyungjun's lyrics? Something about the *shortest distance*.'

'The shortest . . . *what*? Huh?'

'Siwoo hyung!' Hyungjun protested. 'That's . . .'

Sohee looked on in confusion as Hyungjun, visibly flustered, tried to stop Siwoo from saying more. But Siwoo wouldn't be Siwoo if he could be stopped. The words tumbled out of him in a rapid-fire rap.

'Oh, haven't you told her that you'll be working as a lyricist for an OST album?'

'Siwoo hyung, that's not even confirmed yet . . .'

'Oh please. The demo's out. What do you mean *not*

confirmed? You're just too humble. How can you be our social media manager this way? Eh, wait. What's with that projector?' Siwoo jerked his chin at the grey screen on the wall and disappeared as quickly as he came, leaving Hyungjun still stammering. Sohee burst out laughing at his expression.

'Um . . . am I understanding this right? You wrote the lyrics for a song? Wow. I'm curious. If there's a demo, I'd love to listen to it. It's called "The Shortest Distance"?'

'. . . Siwoo hyung didn't even get that right. It's . . . "The Optimal Route",' he sighed.

Hyungjun kept his eyes fixed on the floor as a flush crept up his face. Sohee chuckled as she thought about that rainy summer night. Meanwhile, Yoojin was reading the fairy tale that Sohee had written, with no regard for what was going on.

***

'Soohyuk hyung-nim! I thought you couldn't come!'

Hearing Siwoo's exclamation, Yoojin, who was engrossed in the book, turned. The first she saw was the playful smile hovering at the corner of his mouth, as he spread his arm and gestured to her. But all sounds vanished in that instant. Her gaze was fixed on the person at the entrance, and she blinked.

Standing at the door, in a dark grey cashmere coat, was Min Soohyuk. Just like the first time they'd met, he looked slightly bashful. Yoojin felt as though she'd returned to a past moment. The autumn night on the second-floor terrace, drinking wine mixed with coffee, the stories they shared as they gazed at the occasional glimmer in the sky. The touch of the warm chestnuts, the early morning by the misty lake, the wet fog slowly dissipating and the first rays of light shining down.

Yoojin slowly walked up to Soohyuk. Placing a white paper bag by his feet, he took off his dark blue gloves and turned to Siwoo and Yoojin.

'I'm here to deliver ice wine. It's the perfect dessert to end the night!' Soohyuk grinned at Yoojin, who looked like her soul had yet to return. His low voice was exactly as she'd remembered. Same with his long, slender fingers. But there was something about him that was different. She couldn't quite pinpoint it, but it was as if he'd shed something that had weighed on him and was looking much lighter. Siwoo grinned.

'Hyung-nim, you're wearing glasses today. I've never seen you wear them.'

'Oh. I've been thinking it's time to live a different life, so I went shopping and bought several pairs. Because someone told me that it's not a bad idea to live a new life.'

'Huh . . .'

Confused, Siwoo turned to Yoojin, who burst out laughing. The small gold loop on Soohyuk's gloves caught the light and glinted.

He had a lot to say to Yoojin. But he didn't know where to start. Images flashed across his mind – the reddened eyes, ice wine, the snow day at the cemetery.

***

This was his first time at his mother's grave. It wasn't difficult to find. The weeds hadn't grown over it yet, and his body remembered its way around the cemetery where he had performed the ancestral rites every year. Under the light grey clouds, snow was falling quietly. Soohyuk stared at the grave marker. Until today, he'd refused to come back because he was afraid that he'd finally break down completely and dissolve into unconsolable tears. But now that he was standing in front of his mother's grave on a snowy day, he felt his heart quieten instead. With life, there'd be death. As the snow got heavier, he opened his umbrella and slowly walked down the path, retracing his steps. In the opposite direction, a man was approaching without an umbrella. Soohyuk was about to brush past the man who seemed deep in thought, when the man paused in front of him. Soohyuk stopped and looked up.

It was his father. Flustered, Soohyuk took a step backwards. It felt odd, seeing him alone without his secretary, and without an umbrella in the snow. He hesitated. He wasn't the type to exchange good wishes. It had been at least twenty years since he last wished his father a merry Christmas. But it didn't feel right to casually greet him with a, *Oh, you're here?* After all, this was where the dead were put to rest. His father was carrying a bottle of ice wine. Because it was in a bucket of ice, he could only make out the pattern of the cork and the thin neck, but he recognised it immediately. It was his mother's favourite.

The sight of the bottle triggered something and suddenly, the memories came back to him in a rush. Previously, he'd only remembered his mother listening to jazz songs as she baked, but now, he recalled how his father would bring out a bottle of ice wine after dinner. And until late at night, the two of them would enjoy a drink as they ate the pastry and chatted. He recalled the tender look in his father's eyes, how his mother would occasionally chuckle and smack his arm playfully. Soohyuk realised that his memories of his mother had been incomplete. She wasn't just baking for him and his sister. She was also making desserts that would go well with the ice wine she was sharing with the love of her life.

His mother was always in a good mood when she baked. He used to think that it was because of the delicious aroma of the pastry, but that was only half the truth. His parents had spent their honeymoon in Toronto, visiting the wineries nearby. His mother loved ice wine, so whenever she was feeling down, his father would bring back a bottle. It was a gesture of reconciliation, their fireworks of love.

'Dad . . . is that ice wine?'

His father, who'd been looking silently at him, glanced at the ice bucket. A snowflake fell on top and melted away immediately. He nodded and gave a faint smile.

'Soohyuk-ah . . . you have your mother's eyes.'

Soohyuk could hear the pain in his father's voice. He gazed up, only to see that his father's eyes were red. It was as if he could hear the blood dripping from his heart. The whites of his father's eyes were coloured with longing. This wasn't the face of a cold, aloof entrepreneur, nor was this the perfect, calm, steely god Soohyuk had imagined him to be. This was the face of a man much in love with a woman whom he'd given everything in his life to.

His father loved his mother. When Soohyuk had gone to study abroad without his father's permission, his father hadn't been as angry as he had expected. Now he realised why. It was the same when he had fallen for the scam. Back then, he'd only seen his father's anger. Now, he saw the pain, too. He'd thought his father was judging him, criticising him, but in his own stoic ways, he was showing his love and care for him. On this Christmas Eve, his father was looking at him, seeing the traces of his mother in his eyes. The love of his life, and his son who had inherited her eyes and her kindness . . .

'Son . . . it's Christmas Eve, don't you even have a date?'

Soohyuk snapped out of his reverie and hurried to share

his umbrella. The snowflakes made a dull thud, like tapping on the surface with the blunt tip of a pencil.

'I should be asking why you're here alone on Christmas Eve without an umbrella.'

The corner of his father's lips lifted slightly. Soohyuk smiled, too. His father let out a long sigh. The puff of vapour hung in the air for a second before dissipating.

'. . . Son, don't stay here. Go meet someone you can chat with for hours on end, someone with whom you're comfortable sharing the emotions that sit deep in the well of your heart. After all these years, I've come to see what life is. Even the brightest of success will come to pass, just like euphoria; passion will fade over time. But stories, conversations, will always remain. They'll stay in your heart forever, never to disappear or fade . . .'

His father closed his eyes, letting his sentence trail off. His thoughts were clearly elsewhere. Meanwhile, a gentle breeze blew.

***

Snowflakes landed on Soohyuk's dark blue gloves before melting away, leaving behind a faint trace. It was still snowing at Soyangri Book Kitchen. He picked up the paper bag next to him and turned to Yoojin.

'I know a great place to enjoy the ice wine – shall we?'

The metasequoias looked like two rows of Christmas trees, the thin boughs stretching to form an arch over the road. Because the leaves had all fallen, the snow sat on the bare branches. Not a single footprint dotted the snowcapped ground. The light from the occasional streetlamp coloured the white landscape a warm yellow.

The ice wine was very sweet, with a hint of bitterness at the end. Because they didn't have proper wine glasses, they made do with espresso cups. The dark-coloured alcohol looked like coffee when poured out. At the bench, Yoojin brought the cup to her eye level and turned to Soohyuk.

'My grandpa used to grind coffee beans himself. I was starting university then, and instead of teaching me how to drink, he taught me everything about coffee. Grandpa told me this – *There are moments in life when life feels so bitter that we taste it in our water, but even in such times, there're always deeper layers of flavours within.* When I had my first sip of coffee, I wasn't even sure what I was supposed to be tasting, but after understanding what a good cup of coffee is, I realised that in life, too, there are mysterious, complex flavours hidden behind the bitterness.'

Soohyuk stared at the cup in Yoojin's hands and nodded.

'You're right . . . but I was too busy running away from the bitterness. I didn't know how to acknowledge and accept failures and obstacles. Perhaps that was why I didn't visit my mother's grave on my own, not even once.'

Yoojin stared at his side profile, thinking back to the first snow of the year and how that day, she'd been curious if he was doing well.

'Today, I visited her grave. It was her first death anniversary a few days ago. When I was about to leave, I bumped into my father. He told me to go to someone I can talk to for hours on end. And he told me that stories, conversations, will always remain in our hearts . . .'

Soohyuk paused. Silently, he added: *I realised that I already have someone I want to talk for hours on end with . . .*

Their eyes met, and Yoojin nodded slowly, as if telling him that she was willing to be that person for him.

It was as if she'd stepped into an enormous snow globe. Flakes continued to flutter down. Soohyuk spoke slowly. He told her about the story of the ice wine and his father, the alleyways in Yeonhui-dong and how his mother had run after him, his friend's betrayal, his musical director dream, how work at the company felt meaningless, his mother's death . . .

Yoojin, too, shared her own stories. From growing up being hypersensitive to competition, to burnout, her work at the start-up, the falling-out with her sunbae, watching the sea of clouds and sunrise at Maisan Mountain, the days at Soyangri Book Kitchen . . .

A snowflake landed in the ice wine and melted. The wind blew more snow at them; the world was covered in soft wool. Yoojin took a long sip from her cup.

'. . . Someone told me that plum blossoms are the first to bloom in spring. That it's the first sign that winter is ending. That's why I decided to dress up our plum blossoms for Christmas, hoping that it'll provide some warmth and comfort to those who're having a hard time. Just like how even the bitterest coffee has a deeper flavour to it, I hope everyone will have the strength and courage to welcome a new year.'

A smile spread across Soohyuk's face. He raised his cup, and a crisp clear tinkle rang out as they made a toast. Yoojin returned his smile.

'Merry Christmas.'
'Merry Christmas.'

Yoojin and Soohyuk sat on the bench at the metasequoia-lined road and chatted till late. Over at Soyangri Book Kitchen, a few wild cats prowled the garden as if it was their home. The snow had stopped. As the clouds cleared, the full moon emerged from behind them, casting a dim light on the surroundings. Hanging in clusters on the plum blossom trees were the time capsules that held wishes, heart flutters, lingering regrets and sorrow, lit up by the mini bulbs twined around the tree trunks. The delicious smell of lemon cake drifted by like the clouds in the sky. It was that kind of night.

EPILOGUE 1

TIME OF STARLIGHT AND WIND

In the daytime, Hawaii was dazzling, glamorous, perfect. The sun shone down like a spotlight, as if falling on a superstar surrounded by cheering fans. Above, the sky was a gorgeous blue, decorated with cotton-candy clouds as soft as hotel pillows. It was the kind of place that needed no filters. The air was clear and fresh, the palm trees reaching high up in the sky. Not to mention the posh restaurants everywhere. Da-in thought she'd landed in a paradise somewhere on earth.

Yet, she preferred Hawaii at night. Instead of a glamorous young woman, the island at night felt like a warm-hearted grandmother. From her window, she could hear the gentle sloshing of waves and when she pushed it open, the salty breeze drifted in. She tied her flying strands of hair into a side ponytail and stepped out onto the terrace. The sky was dark; not a single star was in sight. For a moment, dim moonlight shone down before the moon was hidden behind the clouds again. It was eleven at night. From the terrace, she looked out at the ocean in the distance. Waves crashed onto the shore, breaking into white frothy bubbles before retreating, over and over again.

Dear Grandma,

Da-in paused, adjusting her grip on the pen. Emotions welled up in her, as if she'd been swept up by a sudden current. *Give me a little more time*, her pounding heart seemed to tell her. But she couldn't keep pushing it back forever. Her thoughts drifted to the night sky at the book kitchen. Then she looked up again above her. Behind the clouds, the stars must be twinkling, even if they weren't visible right now. Da-in let out a short sigh. For a moment, she listened to the waves, felt the wind on her face. Slowly, she picked up the pen again, as if it were a telephone line connecting her to Grandma.

Grandma, I'm writing from Hawaii. It's nighttime now, and I can hear the waves outside. It's as if I'm back in the mountains in Soyangri, where the wind went whoooosh, and the leaves would rustle in greeting, the foliage shining in shades of green and yellow the way the lake glitters in the sun.

At your hanok, one of my favourite things to do was to listen to the wind and fall asleep on the floor. When I woke up, you'd be next to me plucking bean sprouts or peeling garlic. Sometimes, you were simply gazing at the wind-filled forest or turning to smile at me.

Hearing the waves puts me at ease. Even if the night is dark, as long as I hear the ocean, it's easy to fall into a restful sleep. It's as if I can hear your heartbeat in the gentle rhythm, as though the waves are sending you my regards.

Grandma, I went back to Soyangri the other day. For the first time since you moved to the nursing home. I drove up the winding highway, going round and round until I reached the place you'd loved so much. The hanok has been remodelled into a hanok hotel in the adjacent neighbourhood. The shed where I used to play hide-and-seek wasn't there any longer. Instead, brand-new buildings now occupy the land.

Yet, the winds were still the same. When they went whoooosh, it was as though you were right there, smiling at me. The persimmon trees, too. I remember how you tied the fruits and hung them from the rooftop to dry them out. Do you remember how I tried to climb the trees like a squirrel and fell on my butt instead?

That night, I gazed at the stars in the sky, and time seemed to look back at me. It was as if I was swimming in a small universe. The starlight turned into a quiet column of wind as it whispered to me. It said, I was happy to have loved, grateful to have loved someone so deeply over thousands of sunrises and moonsets, grateful to have created so many cherished memories. And in that moment, I knew. The wind had carried your feelings to me.

I was afraid of saying goodbye to you, as though by doing so, I was surrendering and admitting that you're no longer of this world. I was afraid that without you, there would only be emptiness and loneliness in my life. But in Soyangri, I learnt something. That place is still filled with your presence. You're the sound of the wind, the memories under the sunlight. Time has paused there, and I can always return to relive our memories.

There are also new beginnings there. The old shed is now a small café. Looking at the weathered stones was like seeing another version of you. I'm sure the guests now and in the future will be comforted by the warm touch of the place. As I looked up at the star-speckled sky, I thought of you, how you are now one of the shining stars lighting up the sky. May the books at Soyangri Book Kitchen welcome everyone into the world of stories and words, may the music set them free.

Grandma, I made an instrumental track for you. I didn't use my voice; it doesn't have an addictive hook, a powerful climax. It's a song where I put in my truest self – the music of the mountain winds at Soyangri, the waves in Hawaii, and the stars in the night sky. Grandma, are you listening to it, too? When I recorded it, I prayed that it'd reach you somewhere in the universe.

Grandma, I love you.

Your dearest granddaughter,
Da-in

The waves sloshed and gently receded in response. Da-in didn't cry. Sadness had no place in this warm, peaceful night. Listening to the demo, she drifted off to sleep. It was as if she was lying on Grandma's lap. *How warm.*

EPILOGUE 2

A YEAR AGO TODAY

The automatic glass doors slid open to reveal an impressive lobby. With high ceilings at ten metres tall, it felt as though she was about to enter a large grey box. The low tables by the windows had the effect of making the space feel even more expansive.

Yoojin subconsciously tightened her grip on her purse. Behind her was the bustle of cars, pedestrians and the occasional beeps of the traffic light. For a moment, she looked around, taking in the sights of Teheran-ro, Gangnam, and its fancy skyscrapers. And taking a deep breath, she stepped into the lobby.

'Yoojin, here!' A man stood up and called out to her. It was her sunbae. His colleague, whom she'd been liaising with, also walked forward to greet her.

'Thanks for your hard work,' her sunbae added.

'Same to you, Sunbae, Team Leader Kang. Are you sure you're not having an opening event?'

'Come on, Yoojin, who still does ribbon-cutting ceremonies these days? How old-fashioned! A waste of time and money. Since it's meant to be a reading space, as long as people are using it, that's good enough, isn't it?'

It was the opening day of the private library that Yoojin had helped to curate. Four open shelves towering at seven metres high served to demarcate the library space, and within, the flooring was lined with synthetic grass and decorated with potted plants, recreating the vibes of an indoor garden. Besides cosy single seats, there were also long sofas where the employees could stretch their legs out and read comfortably. The shelves were filled with books from comics to quantum physics titles, but mostly essay collections or light-hearted novels that people could pick up for an easy read.

It was only ten in the morning and already, a couple of employees were in the library browsing the books and holding cups of coffee as they chatted. The three of them stood shoulder to shoulder, like chefs observing if people were enjoying their cooking.

'Everyone, from the president to the employees, has been gushing about how much they like the library,' said Team Leader Kang.

'Wow, really?'

'Of course. They love the name too; it's a perfect complement to the garden vibes.'

Beaming, Yoojin cast a glance at the sign – *A Mindful Walk* – and thought back to Serin's smiling eyes.

'The idea came from one of our staff at the book kitchen. She hoped that even in the heart of central Seoul, there could be a place that allowed people to rest their minds, much like taking a walk around Soyangri.'

Just then, Yoojin's phone pinged. It was a systems notification from the photo gallery: *Tap to see the memories from a year ago.*

Curious, she tapped on it. The first photo that appeared was of Hyungjun and Siwoo holding a banner between them, their windswept hair dancing in all directions. Siwoo was grinning, Hyungjun had his usual poker face on. She swiped left. A sun-drenched book café while they were doing the final checks. A spread of dishes they had cooked for dinner. The star-speckled night sky. As she swiped through the album, her initial nervousness melted away as a tender feeling filled her heart.

Yoojin went back to the photo of Hyungjun and Siwoo. Neither of them would be around when she returned to the book kitchen in the afternoon. Hyungjun was in Seoul. He was going away for at least a couple of months because he'd be busy with an album production project. As for Siwoo, he had taken leave for the first time in a year to go on a trip with his friends and would return the day after tomorrow. But for Hyungjun, it was unclear if he'd come back to Soyangri after this project.

She thought back to the early days when all was uncertain and new. Luckily, everything that they'd worried about didn't happen. Was it to the credit of the wonderful people or the place? The book kitchen that she'd created to fill empty hearts ended up filling her own.

It was the start of a new chapter for her. The past year at Soyangri had brought several changes within her. She wasn't sure if she could call it *growth*, but at the very least, she wasn't the same Yoojin she was a year ago. And that was the same for Siwoo, Hyungjun and Serin.

Yoojin started the car engine. She'd just finished lunch with her sunbae and Team Leader Kang, and it was time to head back to Soyangri. The thought of returning to the book kitchen without Siwoo and Hyungjun felt odd. Passing through the skyscraper forest in Teheran-ro, she turned onto the busy Gyeongbu Expressway. An hour later, she could finally make out the familiar mountain ridges in the distance.

Driving along the narrow, winding highway, she thought, I'm home.

Soyangri had become her home. It was already mid-March, but the mountain peaks were still covered in snow even as the first shoots of green were starting to appear. On the other side, at the foot of the mountain, she could see the outline of Soyangri Book Kitchen, the resting spot she'd built for those who were going through a tough time, a hideout for the weary soul.

Yoojin parked the car and slowly walked towards the buildings. A white Jindo puppy scampered towards her, his tail wagging furiously. She'd adopted Sanchek a month ago – in Korean, the word means *leisurely walk*. Serin came running behind him. She was just about to leash him when he saw Yoojin and made a beeline for her. Glancing into the windows of the book café, Yoojin saw several customers at the tables reading and chatting, like a scene you'd see in a movie.

Right on cue, the scent of the plum blossoms and the snow rode the wind towards her. A sweet, yet distant fragrance. The sun had yet to set, but already, the moon hung high in the sky.

AUTHOR'S NOTE

One night, I was at the airport, waiting for my flight home after a business trip. I sat at the quiet boarding gate and stared up at the full moon. It occurred to me that I was hovering precariously at the edge of life. Just as boarding gates seem to straddle invisible borders, it was as if I could never put down my roots in one place. Neither did I have the courage to cross the boundary and venture beyond. I was always stuck somewhere in between.

That feeling encapsulated my thirties. If life were a flight board, instead of being on schedule, mine would be flashing a series of *delayed*, with a few *cancelled* flights peppered in between. Marriage, career change, work, parenting – each of them was like a deafening wave crashing upon me, never allowing me a quiet moment. In the time others were heading home or boarding a connecting flight to a different part of the world, I was permanently stuck on the waiting list. Perhaps to others, I looked cheery and optimistic all the time, but the fact was that I lived each day of my thirties feeling as though I was hovering on the boundary.

Summer, 2020. Several reasons led me to leave my job, and I started taking on freelance translation projects. Quitting in the middle of a long-drawn-out pandemic felt as though life had shut down for me. I craved something that would connect me to the world, so I found solace in reading voraciously, mostly essay collections and novels. It was a longtime habit of mine, to read whenever I was stressed. Over time, a deep thirst welled up in me. It was not so much a desire to write, but that the thirst wouldn't be quenched until I wrote something. And in the spring of 2021, the year I turned forty, I dived into the world of Soyangri Book Kitchen.

I listened carefully to my worries and anxieties, the messy and complicated thoughts that had plagued me in my thirties as I dreamt of a place that could provide comfort and encouragement to weary hearts. I wrote, with the belated hope that I wished I could've read a novel like this when I was in my thirties. I created the world of Soyangri Book Kitchen, hoping to remember the happy memories in my life. If only I could've read the story in my thirties, perhaps I might've been able to walk through the dark tunnel feeling a little calmer, surer. I only hope that one day, my children will be able to read this when they turn thirty. That was my wish. Like how stars travel a long time to become the light in our eyes, I hoped that someday, my story would be able to reach them.

As I wrote, I grew closer to the folks at Soyangri Book Kitchen, as though I'd been journeying alongside them through the different seasons. As I described the changes in the landscape at every turn of the season, telling the stories of spring, summer, autumn, and winter, I felt as though I was also living those moments myself. I was surprised at how much I enjoyed spending time at the small café in my neighbourhood in the morning, reading or writing my novel. As I looked at the photos of the breathtaking landscape at Maisan Mountain, I imagined how the winds blew in from the forest, the touch of the sunshine . . . And at dusk, when the sun had set and stars glittered in the sky, I thought about how lovely it'd be to share a warm meal and laughter with the people I missed. Before I realised it, the characters in the novel were hanging out, eating, listening to music together, chatting about books over a glass of wine. And I was next to them, joining in their conversations.

Writing my first novel brought me a lot of joy. When I first started, I hadn't quite imagined that others would be reading the story I wrote, so right now, I'm a little nervous. However, if the happiness I felt while penning the novel could be shared, even if just a little, with someone else, I think the story has served its purpose.

Dear reader, I hope that your heart will be touched at the sight of the glittery stars in the sky. When you listen to the summer rain, I hope you'll think of calling a dear friend, and I hope that the bright, melancholy sunshine in autumn will bring back memories of a song you loved. As you turn the pages, may the warm memories in deep slumber find their way back to the surface, and despite the frustrating and at times depressing reality we find ourselves in, it'd be lovely if the book can bring back memories of the beautiful songs, stories and people in your life, warming your heart like the spring sunshine. And if you feel that you're hovering on the boundary, I hope that you can put down your worries for a moment, take the time to recharge and gain the strength to cross over.

Between spring and summer,
somewhere in Soyangri Book Kitchen